PASSAGES OF PECULIARITY

A Collection of Dark Tales

MARK K. MCCLAIN

Passages of Peculiarity by Mark K. McClain

Notice: These short stories deal with subject matter some readers may find offensive to their sensibilities. If this is the case, do not read on. These pages may hold sexual situations, murder, death, foul language, alcohol/drug use, slandering of organized religion, and other difficult themes.

Paperback ISBN: 979-8-9892944-0-4
Ebook ISBN: 979-8-9892944-2-8

Design (Interior / Exterior): Jess LaGreca: jesslagreca.com
Editor: Lisa Wong: lisawongeditorial.com

CONTENTS

WHAT HAVE YOU DONE

Charlie was shaking in bed, but the teen's affliction that July night was not from cold but fear. His teeth pressed into his bottom lip as he sat motionless, listening.

No matter how stealthy the monster tried to be, the floorboards refused to remain silent. The worn hardwood seemed alive as it groaned under the beast's weight. With its guttural-sounding voice, it reached the second floor.

Charlie was born and raised in the house and memorized every noise. By the sounds alone, he knew the animal's location. This skill was crucial in determining which victim the beast would choose on any given night.

He gripped the sheets with sweaty palms and drew them tight to his chest.

"Not tonight," he whispered, summoning what bravery he could. "I won't let it happen again." Cringing at his oath, he cursed, for the words felt hollow and false.

Then, the moment came. If the boards made their familiar groaning sound, the monster would choose him, while a high-pitched squeak meant it had turned down the hallway toward Sarah's room.

His sister was thirteen. It was his job to protect her now. After all, he was a man and could handle himself. Yet, facing the evil presence was difficult at any age.

The floor squeaked, making Charlie mutter another curse. Sarah's doorknob rattled moments before the door opened with shrill protest. Seconds later, low talk drifted down the hall, and though he could not hear the words, he knew the outcome. Sarah's pleading voice came next, rising clear, stirring his feelings of guilt and growing anger.

Charlie sprang from his bed, slid on jeans and a t-shirt, grabbed the thirty-inch Louisville Slugger from his closet, and slunk down the hall. The beast was shushing Sarah to quiet her.

"It's okay," it said. "Relax. Hush now. Hush. You always like this part."

Charlie had heard those reassurances for years. Maybe they finally worked on her. Worse yet, perhaps she just gave up.

Reaching the door, he peeked through the keyhole. Sarah, whose body had filled out in the last two years, stood in a bra and panties as the animal's hands ran over her skin and through her hair. Then, it placed one hand between her legs while moaning with pleasure.

The young man squeezed both eyes shut, trying to summon his courage in hopes of ending the nightmare with sheer willpower. But once he heard the familiar sound of a belt buckle clinking, he cursed softly and returned his eye to the keyhole. His father's pants were on the floor, bunched around his ankles.

This was the moment Charlie had planned for, even dreamed of for years. The animal would pay tonight.

Cautiously turning the knob, he sucked in a quick breath as the one-hundred-year-old metal squealed for an instant. He readied himself.

Throwing his weight against the door, he burst inside and charged with the bat waggling at waist level. He drew back and swung hard, giving a battle cry like a bold, armored knight. The blow struck squarely before his father could utter a sound.

With a howl of pain, the big man dropped, clutching his knee as he cussed and moaned. Charlie wondered if the blow brought back horrible memories of Vietnam. His old man was familiar with agony, having been wounded in action and decorated for bravery.

Though, at present, he didn't seem heroic with his pants twisted around his ankles while he whined like a sissy. On a good day, that was the word he always described Charlie with—sissy. When their father was angry, the insults were far worse.

"You touch my sister again, and I'll kill you. I mean it, you piece of shit," yelled Charlie as his resolve swelled. "You'll never lay a finger, or anything else, on either of us again."

His father laughed as he cradled his knee. "You have big ones. I'll give you that. But when I get off this floor, I'll snap your neck like a dry twig, then throw you out with Saturday's garbage. You just became the enemy, boy!"

"Kill him, Charlie," cried Sarah. "Do it! Or I will. I won't let him put his thing in me again." She reached for the bat but her brother's long arm held her at bay.

"Yes, do it, Charlie," taunted their father in a feminine-sounding voice. His face hardened as his brows pushed closer together. "Go on! Hit me again, sissy boy. You can't do it while I'm looking at you, can you? Don't have the guts, do you, worm?"

After tucking his manhood back into his undershorts, the big man rose, struggling to pull up his trousers while balancing on his one good leg. Standing again, he tested the injury, then glared at his children.

Charlie swallowed hard. His hands were shaking as he met his old man's eyes.

"I'm warning you. If you take one more step, it will be your last. No more purple heart or silver star medals for you this time."

"You arrogant piece of crap," shouted his father. "I've killed better men than you with my bare hands." He hobbled forward, reaching out with two thick hands as his face twisted in anger.

After a quick sidestep, Charlie swung like he had done during last year's baseball championship when he had driven the ball over the fence to win the game. The bat connected with his father's skull in a solid blow. It made a horrible crunching sound. Sarah shrieked, hopped on the bed, then pulled her pillow to her like a protective shield.

The large man impacted the floor face first as blood formed a pool around his head. Crimson liquid oozed onto the hardwood. Charlie hit him again for good measure and to take out years of suppressed hate, then a third time to be sure. The strikes came from high overhead, falling axe-like, like splitting firewood. The blows crushed the war hero's skull.

"Shit! You killed him!" cried Sarah with wide eyes. She slid off the bed to move closer and stare.

"That *was* sort of the idea," he said. "And I warned him, didn't I? Besides, it's not like anyone will give a shit. Who's going to miss him?"

Sarah wiped away the lone tear rolling down her cheek, then threw both arms around her brother's neck. "It's really over."

"No. It's only beginning." Charlie released her. "Get dressed. We need to get rid of him and clean this mess up."

"What about mom?"

Her brother shook his head. "She's either drunk or high again. Most likely passed out on the couch. Her worthless ass is always there."

"What if we get caught? We should've thought this through. I'm really scared."

He rested a reassuring hand on her shoulder. "Me, too." Pushing his chin toward the dresser, he repeated himself. "Get dressed."

Before long, the siblings had the bloody corpse wrapped in old bedsheets and a spare comforter. They dragged their victim down the hall, but the struggle was significant and took longer than imagined.

"I'm sorry," whispered Sarah. "I'm trying. But he's so damned heavy."

Charlie nodded several times in agreement. He tried to sound encouraging. "It's okay. You're doing fine."

After much effort, and as their father's head thumped each step as they dragged his lifeless body downstairs, they passed through the house unnoticed.

Outside, Charlie wiped his brow, then faced his sister. "Stay here. I'll be right back." Sprinting to the barn, he returned on an ATV with shovels fastened to the front rack. He sprang from the seat, tied a rope around the corpse's legs, and secured the loop to the four-wheeler hitch. Checking both ends, he looked at his sister and patted the seat. "Come on. Keep your eyes open and make sure we're not spotted."

"It's the middle of the night," she said, straddling the thick cushion. "Who the hell is going to see us?"

Charlie joined her, then slid his butt toward the handlebars to give her more room. He thumbed the gas lever as her arms encircled his waist.

Off they went into the deep shadows to take the trail he knew by heart. Some two hundred yards later, they dismounted, grabbed their shovels, and dug. The headlights lit the spot.

"Why here?" asked Sarah, taking a breather. "Seems like we could've hidden him better."

"The ground was tilled recently, so it's soft. And it has the worst view around. No shade, no water, nothing. Just what the pervert deserves."

Two long hours passed before the siblings returned home.

Their mother was waiting. She stood leaning against the wall, half-naked, with a cigarette dangling from her lips and a whiskey bottle clutched in one hand. Unkempt hair lay over both shoulders, and her skin was pallid. Wobbling to straighten, as if seeking to regain a sense of lost pride, she eyed her children.

"Where the hell have you two been? It's pitch-black outside. Are you two just coming home?"

Her voice is slurred. She's drunk as usual. Worthless cow!

"Answer me, you little piece of shit," she said, pointing a shaking finger at Sarah. "Where have you been? Were ya' out showing some boy a good time?"

"Leave her alone," cried Charlie. "She doesn't need your mouth. This is all your fault, anyway!"

Their mother forced air through her lips to make a disgusted sound. "You always were an idiot," she retorted. "You never know what you're talking about. You're a blamer, Charlie. You always have been. Nothing's ever your fault. Is it? There's always someone to blame."

"He's right!" said Sarah. She moved before her brother as if deflecting the accusations. "Any *real* mother would have protected us."

"Protected you from what, stupid girl?" The cigarette fell from her mouth as she staggered forward to steady herself against the couch. She waved her free arm in the air. "You've got a nice house, food to eat, and parents that love you. What else do you want, ya' spoiled brat?"

"The house is a shit hole. We barely eat, and maybe we're tired of our own father screwing us whenever he feels like it," snapped Charlie. He pointed a stiff finger at her. "You're supposed to protect us. I hate you!"

"You ungrateful weasel! Your father's the man of the house. It's his right to take what he wants. You should be happy he shows you love."

"Love!" cried Sarah. "Bedding down your own children is not love, dumbass!"

"How dare you!" Their mother raised a hand and lurched forward again.

Charlie readied for another attack, but it was unneeded. Their mother stumbled and fell, shattering the bottle into sparkling shards as the whiskey seeped between the floorboards to disappear. The siblings never moved. They only stared.

"We are your parents. We gave you life, you ungrateful bastards. You'll do whatever we say. If your father wants to give you some lovin', then take it," she said, hauling her shaking frame upright once more. "Do what you're told and keep your mouth shut. Worthless, I tell ya'."

"You're the worthless one," snapped Charlie. He shook his head in disgust, then spit on the floor as he guided Sarah toward the stairs. "Come on. I've heard enough from her noise box," he said.

"I really despise her," she murmured. "It wouldn't bother me if she disappeared, too."

"I know, right? But she's the least of our worries right now. Let's go clean up our mess."

As the siblings plodded upstairs, their mother continued her rant in the background.

Two more hours ticked away as the pair scrubbed, mopped, and wiped the blood from the room, halls, and stairs.

Charlie finally plopped on the edge of his bed, exhausted. "I'm taking a shower," he said before sighing. "We need to sleep. The sun will be up soon, and I'm already worn out. Come on. I'll walk you to your room."

Sarah started. "You're kidding, right? How am I going to sleep in the room you just killed our father in?"

Her brother rested a hand on her shoulder. "You can always sleep here. We can share a bed like when we were little. It'll be fun."

"I remember, but that was like centuries ago." She smiled thinly. "I haven't had any happy memories like that in a long time."

"I'll go fetch some of your clothes." He hugged her. "It'll be okay. You'll see. Besides, it's done. We can't take it back."

"I wouldn't even if we could," said Sarah. "He deserved what he got."

"Yes, he did." *But I wonder how long it will take before Mom realizes he's missing. Then what? With luck, she'll be so stoned she won't figure it out for months.*

Dull yellow light crept through the window as Charlie sat bolt upright. Sarah was screaming. The noise filled his ears.

"Wh . . . wh . . . what the hell is wrong?" he cried, facing her. "What are you hollerin' about?" He jammed both fists against his eyes to massage them as he attempted to force himself awake.

She pointed a stiff finger across the room. "Look!"

He gazed at a man occupying the plush armchair, casually staring back. The stranger nodded politely.

Shocked into action, Charlie sprang from bed, lunged for the closet door, and groped inside its depths for his trusty bat. He emerged to meet the man's eyes.

"Who the hell are you?" asked Sarah, her voice wavering with fright.

Charlie charged with his Slugger held high, but the man raised a hand to stop him.

"Haven't you already done enough damage, murderer?" asked the stranger. With a sweep of his arm, two chairs appeared. "Please sit down. No one wants to bargain while they're uncomfortable." He raised a finger in the air and smiled. "After all that digging and cleaning, you two must be famished." Another arm motion brought end tables filled with food and drink. "I assure you, it's safe. I haven't come to watch you roll about, frothing at the mouth while poison agonizingly kills you. That would be rather idiotic, wouldn't it?" He chuckled. "Exciting, to be sure, but idiotic nonetheless."

The siblings exchanged confused glances.

Who is this guy? And how did he do all that? Magic? Charlie shook his head. *Nah, that's not even real. No one can do that fairy tale stuff. This must be a dream.* He cast aside those questions and focused on the actual problem. *There's a stranger in his house, one who may have seen something.* Resolve rose as he gripped the wood tighter, wondering if this man needed to die to protect their secret.

The intruder's handsome, chiseled features and deep, smooth voice made him a powerful presence. He appeared fit, impeccably dressed, and clean-cut by all standards. Whether it was a dream or some bizarre hallucination, Charlie couldn't decide. Still, several ugly scenarios ran through his young mind.

Sarah moved to one chair and sank into its depths to sit wide-eyed and still.

"My sister asked who you are. You need to answer. And how did you get into our house?"

"And if I don't answer? Are you going to kill me, too?" The fellow's eyes narrowed as if presenting a challenge. No response came in return.

"W . . . w . . . what killing?" stammered Sarah before recanting her question. "Fine. How did you know? Did you see us?"

"Dear Sarah, I know everything. Otherwise, I wouldn't be very good at what I do," he said, pausing to sip his drink. "I must openly confess my love of coffee. What a wonderful invention you humans have here."

"What are you? Plus, what's the crack about humans?" Charlie's anger was on the rise. "You look no different than us." He inclined his head toward the food. "You're not special just because you do fancy tricks. Seriously, I don't know where you came from, who you are, how you got here, or what—"

"Do shut up and sit down," interrupted the stranger. The velvet sound of his voice disappeared for a quick moment. "We won't get anywhere with you making empty threats. There's no need to play hero again." He paused to tap his cheek. "Do you know you're very much like your father? Wouldn't you agree? I know because I've watched him for some time. He had trouble with his temper, too. And I notice you are a rather angry, violent young man, as well."

Charlie bristled at the insult. He opened his mouth to speak, but Sarah spoke first.

"My brother wasn't playing hero! He saved me."

"True enough, in some ways. You obviously gave your dear old dad what he had coming. I bet it felt good! Killing the one who abused you all these years must have felt like a weight lifted from your shoulders."

"But I didn't plan on killing him," blurted Charlie. "He came at me, and I . . . I . . ." his voice trailed into silence.

"I believe the words you're looking for are easy to come by, boy.

Repeat after me, 'I caved his skull in.' Go on, say it." Their eyes met. "Just admit what you've done."

Charlie's mouth fell open as he stared, dumbfounded. His thoughts felt thick and slow to form.

Their guest huffed with discontent. "Please, close that thing. You'll start catching flies." He paused to shift in his seat. "Not to mention, it's rather bizarre looking."

Charlie finally lowered into the chair beside his sister. He glanced at her, then faced the intruder. "You're not even real. This is a stupid dream. I knew from the moment you did this." He jerked a thumb toward the tables. "No one can make stuff appear. And no one saw us last night. No one."

The man snorted. "Oh, I'm quite real." Extending a hand, he inclined his head toward it. "You can feel for yourself if it will quell your confusion. However, you're free to believe whatever you wish."

"Stop this shit," demanded Charlie. He pounded his fist into his thigh. "What, are you supposed to be the devil or something?"

After a light chuckle, the stranger settled into a smile. "I've always hated that title. Did you know Christians came up with that nonsense? Before they came along, the word never existed. I can't understand why they always portray me with a pointed tail and horns. It's bothersome if you think about it. I think I'm rather handsome, wouldn't you say?" After another sip of coffee, his tone turned more serious. "To answer, I am older than time. I have seen the universe contract with the passing of life and expand from glorious creation. I am the thing humans fear but cannot escape. I am immortal. I am death. The Underworld god, if it pleases you."

"That's ridiculous. Do you—" began Charlie.

"Why are you here, then?" interrupted Sarah, scowling at Charlie to halt his arguing. "Shouldn't you be taking our dad away and leaving us alone?"

"It doesn't work that way." The intruder straightened his clothes and adjusted both sleeves. "Let me expand my story a bit. Once your sad little race began assigning names and distorting my image, I grew to become all the terrible things that go bump in the night. Krampus, Ahriman, Satan, Anubis, Kali, and more. I am all of them." After politely dabbing his mouth with a linen napkin, he rubbed his chin. "I've always hated 'devil' though. That word bothers me a great deal. Maybe it's because I'm not such a bad sort. I'm just doing a job."

"What should we call you?" asked Sarah. "You haven't told us your name."

"Forget that! Enough with the games. Why are you here?" asked Charlie.

Their visitor rose with deliberateness and began to pace. "I assure you this is no game. You've committed murder and now your soul belongs to me." He stopped and inclined his head to Sarah. "To answer your question, sweet young thing, you may call me Anubis. He is my favorite of all my roles. However, I do enjoy this human form. It looks and feels unique, nothing like the crazy red fellow with a tail and pitchfork, right? How absurd is that nonsense? Imagine—using a false image to spread fear and keep people in line. Bah!"

"Then, show yourself as Anubis," said Sarah, her tone sounding firm.

"He can't, and you know it. He's a fraud."

"I wouldn't want to scare you, would I? But if you insist and if it will put your brother's doubts aside . . ." Anubis morphed. With long jackal-like ears and slender muzzle, his dark canine form sat atop a muscular, human-shaped body, one as equally black as the night. With a golden ankh around his neck, a crook in one hand, and a flail in the other, his eyes flashed white as he stared at the teens.

"Much better. Isn't it?" the god asked in a low, graveled voice. Both eyes flashed again as they settled on Charlie. "I have judged your soul, which has failed the test."

"What does that mean?" Charlie looked away, unable to meet the intense stare.

Anubis reverted to human form. "It means while you await your next life, should the great Osiris choose to grant you one, your afterlife will be . . . let's say . . . unpleasant."

"You mean he'll burn in Hell? Is that what you're saying?" asked Sarah.

Taking his seat, Anubis chuckled and waved a dismissive hand. "There is no such place. Yet another absurd Christian concept to keep their followers in line. Fear of Hell and trepidation over their own God keeps them terrified. Organized religions want sheep, not free thinkers. Churches hang Hell and sin over their worshippers' heads like the Sword of Damocles." Leaning forward, he waved a hand again.

Horrible images filled the room, playing like a twisted movie on a large screen. Humans roamed freely as rotten flesh fell from their bones. Some ran about as flames engulfed them, others were missing limbs, and some kicked and fought against the noose encircling their necks as life slowly drained from them. There were far more atrocities than Charlie ever imagined. Oddly, several looked unaffected.

"How are *they* tortured?" asked Charlie, pointing to the latter.

No sooner had the words escaped his lips when a woman laughed hysterically and threw herself to the ground to stuff dirt in her mouth before swallowing. A stout man hurled himself from a building's edge to splat on a concrete sidewalk many stories below like a bug hitting a windshield. The moment replayed itself as the man repeatedly leaped to his death.

"Madness is a perfect torture that dwells within us all. It's only a question of how you contain it, for you can never fully control it. Some say you live in a version of Hell, even now. Has it ever occurred to you that your precious planet is a version of Hell? Don't you agree? Seriously, look at your lives. In addition, you'll find out soon enough if the legends of eternal torture are true. Murderer."

"Charlie was only protecting me," said Sarah. She clasped both hands together pleadingly. "Mr. Anubis, you can't take him."

"Ah, but your reasoning is not relevant. Your precious big brother killed because he wanted to."

"That's bullshit!" cried Charlie. "I really didn't want to do it!"

"Then ask yourselves why you simply didn't run away. Why not request help from a relative? Go to the police, a priest, a shaman, or someone you trust. Anyone! You've had years to seek a resolution. Yet here we are." Anubis pointed to the young man, but his stern gaze went to Sarah. "Instead, Charlie murdered your father! Didn't he?"

She cast her eyes to the floor and nodded.

Anubis smiled thinly, then continued. "He beat him to death with a baseball bat." The god smiled wider. "Admittedly, that was the perfect touch. Nicely done. In today's world, everyone wants to solve their issues with guns. That's for cowards. Knives are fine if used properly. But it takes a special kind of fervor to kill up close while vengeance rips at your heart—to smash their brains into mush. I admire that part of you."

"And if I refuse to go?" asked Charlie. "You can't take me." *Why am I even talking to this thing? It's a stupid dream.*

Anubis exhaled heavily. "Do you seriously believe you have a choice?" With another hand gesture, Charlie vanished, though his terrified screams reverberated from a place unseen. Seconds later, the teenager was back, curled on the floor in a fetal position, sobbing.

Sarah rushed to his side. "What happened? Where did you go?"

His mouth opened when he raised his head, but no words came. Charlie's eyes bulged, and his skin was sallow. His body shook and twitched in spasms as he sat upright with Sarah's aid. Her comforting hands rested on his back, but his shaking did not subside.

Charlie squeezed his eyes shut, hoping the nightmarish visions would go away. Anubis had shown him scenes of his father's murder. Only this time, Charlie enjoyed the act, laughing as he repeatedly struck his victim's skull. Soon, the molester's brains were oozing slush, much of which splattered on the young man's clothing. The scene played like a sick horror movie.

Charlie faced Anubis. "I'll do anything you ask. Don't make me go back there."

"What did you do to him?" cried Sarah.

"I merely showed him what his new life will soon entail. I'm sure it was unpleasant enough. After all, that is the idea of punishment. It's unfortunate your race only knows hate, intolerance, and immorality. If you were more peaceful and learned to love one another, my job would be much less tedious. But, as it is, your vicious cycle will never end."

"Please, I beg you," implored Charlie.

Anubis laughed again, harder this time. "Very typical. *Now* you beg, stupid human. It's all you flesh-things know how to do when trapped, and realization sinks into your tiny brains of what awaits. Why is it when you have absolutely nothing to offer, mortals insist on saying they will do anything I ask?" His eyes flashed red. "I promise you will do exactly as I ask. First, you will pay the ultimate price—your soul."

"No, wait!" Sarah shouted, sticking her slender arm out to ward off the god. "There has to be another way."

"I came for a soul, and with a soul, I shall leave. There is no other way, young lady."

Sarah's brain worked rapidly. "You mentioned a bargain," she continued, squeezing Charlie's arm. "You said no one wants to bargain while they're uncomfortable. Well, we're uncomfortable. Take another soul instead. Just don't take my brother, please!"

Anubis tilted his head to one side and raised an eyebrow. "Whose then? Whose soul are you willing to trade, if not that of your dear, sweet, murderous brother? It seems you are not very knowledgeable at the concept of trading."

"Take our mother," she yelled as her grip tightened. "She's worthless. In fact, she doesn't even know we exist."

Shifting in his seat, Anubis inhaled sharply, then smiled. "By the gods, you *are* ruthless. I like you. We could be friends."

"Yes, take our mother," agreed Charlie. "She's nothing to us."

"She gave you life," countered the god. "Doesn't that mean anything?" With a twirl of his finger, his coffee steamed. He took a sip.

"Then again, you've already slaughtered your father, so why not add her to the list."

The siblings recoiled at his bluntness.

"She always reminds us that she gave us life," said Sarah. "But that's all she ever did, the miserable drunk. She owes us for the twisted life she put us through, not the other way around. Now she can make up for it by saving Charlie."

"Please. I'll do—" began Charlie.

Anubis interjected. "Don't you dare say it, or I'll send you back this instant." His eyes flashed again.

Charlie clapped a hand over his mouth and shook.

"Let me understand you," began the god, switching to his deified state. "You are willingly sacrificing your mother's soul to my care for eternity in exchange for your brother's release?"

The siblings nodded in unison. "We don't need her. She's nothing but a shell. Take her," insisted Sarah. "We'll do fine on our own. I don't know how, but we will. Charlie and I can find jobs."

"Sarah's right. She's a burden. Besides, it's not like things are great with her around. Anything will be better than the life we've had so far."

Extending a muscular arm, the god growled an animalistic sound as he pointed at Charlie.

"Say it for it to be so," said Anubis. "Speak your wishes."

Charlie stood, wobbling at first, then pushed his chest out. "Take our mother as payment for my soul, then leave."

The god snapped his fingers. "Done! "Now, my little murderous pair, I shall leave you to your short lives. Do remember that no one escapes my reach. We will meet again, and you will not be as lucky next time." He looked probingly at Charlie. "Then whose life will you bargain with? Perhaps you will sacrifice your sister?"

Charlie's eyes shot wide as Sarah backed away. He shook his head. "He's saying that to drive a wedge between us. I just saved you! Why would I do such a thing only to double-cross you? Don't let him poison your mind."

"Ah, I love family time," said Anubis. "Nevertheless, I must be off. There are plenty of others who must make choices this day. My work is never done. See you soon, my violent little cherubs. Of that, I'm certain." After a practiced bow, he vanished.

"At least he left the food," joked Sarah as she lowered into the chair again.

Charlie nodded. "Yeah, it's like winning some weird game show prize."

"Now what?"

"I don't know." Charlie shrugged. "Maybe we'll wake up and realize this was a dream."

Sarah frowned and shoved his shoulder. "We're well past that point. You know damn well this is real. We're not sharing a dream, you goof."

"How do we know Anubis kept his word? Mom could still be downstairs stoned out of her mind. All he did was snap his fingers."

Charlie jumped up, sprang into the hall, raced down the creaking stairs, and into the living room. His sister was mere steps behind.

They stopped in stunned silence. The house was empty and spotless. It looked brand new. No sign remained their mother had ever been present. The soiled clothes, crumbled newspapers, empty whiskey bottles, drugs, and paraphernalia, were gone.

Still shocked by the sight, Charlie jumped as a loud knock echoed behind them. The siblings exchanged uneasy glances.

"Who can that be? We never get company."

"I have no idea." He shuffled to the door and cracked it open. Blood drained from his face. His insides knotted. "Sheriff Clements. It . . . it's good to see you."

"Likewise, Charlie. Listen, we need to discuss an odd thing that happened this morning." The sheriff pushed his chin forward. "Mind if I come in for a spell? It's already gettin' on the hot side out here."

Charlie's eyes widened. "Oh, sure. Where are our manners!" Stepping aside, he opened the door wider and swept an arm toward the living room.

Clements crossed the threshold to look the teens over. "Well, look how big you two are getting. Charlie, I swear you've grown three inches since I saw you at school last month. My goodness, you two are sprouting up fast." His gaze covered Sarah as she neared. "Why, just last week, you both were this tall." He held a level hand just above his waist.

Her laugh sounded uneasy. "We haven't gotten out much lately. Daddy doesn't let us go many places. We certainly didn't spring up overnight." She gave another nervous laugh.

"True enough. You know, I almost forgot why I'm here." His eyes covered the living room. "Say, this place is mighty clean. Your mama must be awfully busy to have this place shinin' like a new penny. I've never seen it like this before. By the way, is she about? She'll be wantin' to hear this news, too. Plus, I've got some questions for her."

"No, Sir. She was gone when we woke up," lied Sarah.

"Any idea where she went?" asked Clements.

Sarah shook her head.

"You said you had a story, Sheriff. Can we hear it?" Charlie eased himself onto the loveseat as he pushed panic deep inside.

Sarah dashed to the kitchen to return with a tall glass of ice water. The cubes tinkled like a wind chime as she shuffled forward. She placed it on the end table as the sheriff lowered into their father's favorite recliner.

"Like Charlie said, forgive our lack of manners. We just never have visitors."

"That's so kind, young lady. Thank you much," said Clements with a respectful nod.

"The story?" questioned Charlie again. His nerves felt frayed.

Clements eyed the impatient teen over the glass edge. "Sure enough." He set the drink down and smiled. "Old Mr. Filbert next door lost his dog, Sparky, yesterday. The critter just vanished."

An odd silence fell as the sheriff paused. Charlie's innards knotted again, like the feeling before he pukes. Vomit rose in his throat.

The young man knew the sheriff wasn't stupid, even if he pretended to be at times. He had been to their house before when locals complained about hearing shouting or seeing momma lying out in the front yard, drunk and unconscious. This time felt no different—like he was probing for answers in his usual way.

"Aw, the poor thing may be lost and scared," said Sarah with genuine concern. "I hope he finds him soon enough."

"That's nice, Sarah. But not to worry. Filbert went out searchin' and thankfully found that sweet ol' brown dog."

"Well, that's a happy ending," said Charlie, aiming to sound pleased.

Clements snorted. "Not exactly." He leaned forward and rubbed his thick hands together. "Seems ol' Sparky wandered onto your place, sniffed around a bit, then began digging."

Charlie's world quickly spun out of control. Vomit rose once more as he choked it down again. Glancing at Sarah did not help. She looked sickly and near a faint.

"Anyway," continued Clements, "Filbert called the station and began ranting about a dead body buried here. Of course I went and looked. And guess what! I found yur' daddy out there with his skull bashed in. Even now, my team is lookin' for evidence and all that technical stuff." He leaned back into the thick cushions and met Sarah's nervous stare. "You two have any idea how your father wound up dead and buried in the backyard?"

"N . . . n . . . no, Sheriff." Sarah thrust her face into her hands and began to cry and sniffle. "He's dead! Are you sure?"

Is she faking or having a damned breakdown? Is she going give us up?

"Maybe it was our mom? She did disappear, you know? Maybe she did him in, then hightailed it out of here," blurted Charlie.

Tension filled the air, clawing and scratching at the siblings like a living beast.

Clements is putting all of this together! He knows! Maybe we should tell the story. No one could blame us for doing it. I mean, he was molesting us for years. Think of something, you idiot!

"Say, that's a mighty good observation, son. You could make a fine officer." Clements scratched his bearded chin. "Look here, if there's something you kids want to talk about, now's the time. Cuz' you know we'll catch who did it. Evidence never lies."

"We really don't know anything," said Sarah. "I wish we could be of more help."

"Well, you two may need to come down to the station for a bit. There are a few things to go over. For the record, ya' understand."

Damn it! If we leave, we're never coming home. This fool will find a reason to lock us up. Sarah can't take much more and I'm not going to prison for the rest of my life.

"Excuse me, Sheriff," said Charlie. "I really need to go to the bathroom. I'll be right back. I won't take but a minute."

Clements chuckled. "Well, I can't stand in the way of something that important. You go right ahead."

Clements can kiss my ass. This has gone far enough.

True to his word, Charlie wasn't gone long. He crept downstairs and slunk toward the living room. Sarah met his eyes, watching her brother approach. She drew in a quick breath.

Panicked, her brother shook his head and held a finger to his lips, pushing them forward in a silent shush. *The son-of-a-bitch knows we did it! And I can't have that.* The bat went high into the air.

Sarah gasped and covered her mouth with both hands.

"Are you alright?" asked Clements, leaning forward. He peered behind him, but it was too late.

The moment Sarah screamed, a crack filled the room as Charlie hit another homerun. The sheriff's body fell from the chair, careening off the coffee table's edge to thud on the floor.

Sarah stared at Charlie standing over the body, bat in hand. They exchanged uneasy glances.

"What have you done?" she muttered.

THIEVES

The evening arrived with a mournful breeze and starless sky. Deep within the thick forest of King's Wood, a lone screech owl hooted from a nearby branch. The winged predator steadily surveyed the surrounding area for an unsuspecting meal.

Due to the heavy rainfall two days prior, the ground was more pliable than Elle predicted. While Balik and Alaric's shovels quickly moved soil, the petite, blonde-haired woman fidgeted. This was the third grave they pilfered that night and were yet to be rewarded with more than worthless trinkets. She kept an uneasy watch as the men dug, only stepping forward when she heard a familiar, resonating thump of the blade atop the casket.

Alaric, a tall, handsome man with a rounded European chin, smiled. "Finally," he said, setting aside his shovel to wipe away the dirt. "Let's see what we've found."

Elle begrudgingly peered into the hole. She disliked graveyards and thievery, but the need for money drove her pilfering. She could no longer afford the luxury of giving in to her morals.

Aside from economic gain, she only accompanied her friends because they trusted her instincts and pleaded with her to participate. She knew exactly why they needed her. It was well known she had been aware of certain things from an early age. Strange things. Some called her evil, witch, sorceress, or other unkind names, but she cared little about their labels or judgments.

Balik, the shorter, more muscular of the two men, wedged deeper into the hole to gain leverage as they swung open the lid. His forehead beaded with sweat as he swiped long black hair from his eyes. A small gasp escaped him at the sight of the contents.

The deteriorating corpse lay decorated in all its elegance. Straightaway, Balik went for the lumpy vest pocket. Elle's eyes grew round at every treasure he produced—a fine watch, gleaming necklaces, multiple rings, and several silver coins came into her grasp. Ensuring the pocket was empty, Balik rummaged the rest of the coffin.

"Oi! This fella was done up pretty enough," said Alaric as he helped relieve the cadaver of its previous earthly possessions. "We should get some—" He stopped mid-sentence as his fumbling led to a unique, shiny black ring. The distinctive treasure circling a rotten finger was more valuable than the others. He knew that bit from experience. After all, this was not the first grave they had burgled.

Wiping it clean, he whistled. "Hullo there, my beauty." With a quick motion, he tossed it into Elle's hands. "Keep this separate. We're not sellin' that one. You can keep it as your part of the loot if ya' want." He gave a sly wink before going back to work.

She nodded, examining the dark trinket with a sense of wonder. It was far different than any valuable they had ever discovered, and considering the extent of their previous ventures, that was saying a lot.

"It's quite lovely." She slipped it on her finger. *Perfect fit*, she thought, patting it softly. "Yes, indeed, you're all mine."

Alaric cleared his throat for attention. "A boost up, if ya' please," he said, extending an arm.

Elle pulled both men from the hole in turn. They rapidly brushed off, then plopped onto the ground to divide the copious plunder into their small bags.

"Let's hit some more tonight. We've got plenty of time," said Balik excitedly, eyeing the next grave. "I'm thinkin' this haul could make us rich. Great stuff, this is."

"Hold on," said Elle, pointing to the ugly remnants of their mischief. "We should fill these holes back in right and proper."

"Are you daft? I want treasure, not more manual labor," complained Alaric.

"It's not right," she grumbled. "We've already robbed them. The least we can do is show some respect by filling in our handiwork."

"That's total bollocks! Come on," grumbled Balik, "we're wastin' time."

Rapidly collecting their gear, they headed toward another random headstone. "This one works as good as any," said Alaric, jamming his shovel into the ground before pushing it deeper with his foot. Balik joined in with his spade.

Elle stood watch again, but as the men hefted up lumps of dirt, a compulsive need thrummed within her. Her hand tingled. Curious, she lifted her new ring to eye level. Her gaze danced over strange golden characters engraved on the black band. They had not been there earlier. Enthralled, she ran her fingers over each shape.

"I wonder what these mean," she said, stroking the unique lines. Neither of her mates responded, let alone heard her voice. Her eyes went to them. Watching them huff with exertion, she frowned. "I wish we knew where more treasures were instead of playing this guessing game. We may find nothing here."

Without warning, she shrieked as the ring grew warm and glowed with soft blue light. Balik and Alaric rounded toward her unusual sound.

"Keep it down, ya' bloody fool. We're already takin' a chance," snapped Balik. "I don't want to get caught. I wouldn't look good behind bars."

Alaric laughed. "Ya' don't look good now, mate." After another laugh, he climbed from the shallow hole, dusting off his trousers again. He faced Elle. "What's going on?"

She raised a shoulder. "I . . . I . . . I don't know, really. I was admiring the ring, and it started to glow. I swear I didn't do anything to it."

The men exchanged skeptical looks. Elle huffed at them. Blowing a short breath past her lips, she retraced her steps, reiterating how the piece had come to life after her wish.

"What's all this about?" asked Balik, his gaze fixed ahead. "Take a look there!" He pointed.

The others followed his extended arm to where several gravesites pulsed with luminescent blue light.

"What the bloody hell is that?" questioned Elle, moving to inspect the nearest glowing plot. She looked at her hand where the ring still pulsed. An idea instantly took hold.

"Dig here," she said firmly.

Balik balked. "Whatever for? Just because some freaky light is shinin' on—"

Alaric waved him off as he interrupted. "She's right. You know she's got a nose for this sort of weird stuff. Do what she says unless you can explain any of it." Snatching up his shovel, he advanced to the new site and jammed the steel into the earth again. "Come on, you lazy sot. Help me."

Balik's complaints soon morphed into howling joy as the trio fleeced another grave before quickly moving on to others that glowed. On the fourth one, despite the pair's incessant shoveling noises, Elle turned her ears toward the woods. She stepped toward the darkened forest, listening intently. Something was amiss. Leaning closer to the trees, she thought a voice was there—no, a moaning, in the air.

"This night better not turn into some creepy movie scene," she muttered as a chill raced down her spine. She shivered unwillingly.

"Did you say something?" asked Balik, taking a break to gain his breath.

Elle shook her head, but her stare remained fixed ahead. "I just thought . . . oh, never mind."

"Gettin' a bit freaked out, are ya?" asked Alaric. "You're always jumpy when we treasure hunt."

Another familiar thump distracted her. Balik swung open another coffin down in the hole to reveal much of the same—a small trove of valuable coins, fine jewelry, and expensive knickknacks. "Elle, you're amazing. I'm never doubtin' you again," he cried.

"Ya' sure made this one out quick enough," chimed in Alaric. "Pretty soon, you can afford some new tattoos after we cash this haul in. There'll be a good bit to spare, too."

Elle jumped from fright as the sound returned. This time, much closer. She backed away from the forest's edge, heading deeper into the graveyard. "We should really leave here."

Her words came out softly before an urge to flee took control. Something gripped her heart, filling her with alarm, but the sensation did not originate from within. It rose from a place she could not comprehend, let alone name its source. Evil was at work, she thought.

"We should go, *now!*" she insisted, louder this time.

"I'm not goin' any place," argued Balik, holding up the glimmering loot. "We're gonna' be rich."

"I mean it," she urged, her voice tilting higher with every word. "We need to go! Right now."

"Give it a rest," griped Alaric, looking tired and frustrated. "He's right. Look at all the stuff we can sack from here." Noticing her distress, he rolled his eyes and set aside his shovel. "Fine. Tell me what it is this time? What's bugging you?"

Elle's face went warm. "I have no bloody idea. But we're not alone. Something is here. Watching."

Balik made absurd ghostly sounds and waved his arm about in the air. "Was it like that?" he asked mockingly.

She frowned at him. "Shut your face and dig, will you! I want to get out of here with a bit of speed."

They resumed, carrying on into the night with one grave after another bearing riches beyond their expectations. Finally, a greying sky forced a halt to the thievery. Dawn hurriedly spread over the eastern horizon as they loaded their take into the motor's boot.

Elle's distraction returned, growing stronger. She took no pleasure in packing up the sacks of jingling treasure this time. Something was still amiss. Yet, the sight and sounds of their spoils enticed her. She grew conflicted, deciding whether to listen to her instincts and never return or revisit the site for a chance at significant financial gain.

Regardless of her choice, she knew an energy or force beyond her comprehension had awakened. It was coming. She prayed to the gods it did not seek her. Warning her partners proved pointless. They would not listen to her pleas to abandon the night's raid or care about her forewarning. When loot was involved, it always had a way of removing all semblances of reason or fear.

They piled inside, started the engine, and headed down the road.

"The groundskeeper won't be in 'til Tuesday since tomorrow is a proper holiday, so we're comin' back tonight before he discovers our handiwork," said Balik, lighting a cigarette.

Elle coughed as she rolled down the window. "That is a disgusting habit!" she snarled, waving her hand in front of her face. "Why don't you do that later!"

Alaric, his face visible in the rearview mirror, flicked his eyes up to glance at Elle in the backseat. "Look," he began, ignoring the grey cloud of smoke encircling his head like a halo, "this is our best haul ever. Tonight will be the end of it for a long bit. I promise. By then, we'll have enough to live like royals. Deal?"

The proposition was tempting. Elle considered it. Then, in a moment of terror, she instinctively gripped the back of the driver's seat with strength. Ahead, a silhouette had materialized on the road.

Shrill sounds erupted from her throat. "Look out!" she screamed.

All eyes went forward. Directly before them stood a shabbily dressed man, seemingly unphased by the speeding vehicle coming for him. He looked thin and pale and wore only one shoe. Flesh hung in layers from his bones. One eye was absent from its socket. Greying hair hung down like thick, rotten rope, swaying gently in the breeze.

Even with a quick jerk of the wheel, Alaric could not avoid the decaying man. But no impact came as the trio braced themselves, gripping the doors and pushing their feet flat on the floorboards. The motor sped past. The vision had vanished.

In his attempt to avoid an accident, Alaric oversteered. Elle bit back another scream as the car flew from the road to plunge into a nearby ditch. Balik's head smacked the window hard, opening a gash across his scalp. Alaric's body snapped forward, breaking his nose on the steering wheel. Blood sprayed over the fractured windshield and down his shirt. Elle grunted as the seatbelt yanked tight, digging into her ribs and chest, but it could not stop her face from impacting the front seat. The collision dazed her.

Agonized groans filled the cab as the men clumsily tried to slow their bleeding. Elle, still confused, opened the rear door to fall upon the ground. Crawling on her hands and knees to lean against a high dirt back, she clutched her stomach, wondering if the restraint had damaged her internally. Blood spurted from her mouth, followed by a grimace. *I think my ribs are broken.*

"Is everyone good?" asked Alaric with a nasal voice as he freed himself. He yanked free a kerchief and jammed the corners in his nose to halt the crimson flow.

"What the bloody hell just happened," spat Balik. He yanked off his jumper to ball it up, placing it against his forehead to staunch the bleeding. "Was there a bloke standin' in the road?"

"Thank the gods I wasn't the only one who saw that thing!" huffed Elle, struggling as her damaged ribs made each breath painful.

Fear lurked in her heart as she drew in shallow breaths. Pain riddled each lungful. More blood ejected as she coughed, helping scatter her already skittish thoughts. She would have rather faced rattling chains, disgustingly ugly beasts, or otherworldly ghouls than such a sinister sight. The man looked like a physical representation of the awful instinct she had ignored all night. She was convinced he had come from another realm—the undead.

Before she could voice her idea, her partners stumbled to their feet. Pressing a hand to her ribs, she limped toward them as they maneuvered around the twisted remnants of their motor.

"Let's get our pickings buried," said Balik. "We don't need the bobbies coming to investigate and asking questions. Hell, they may even nick our loot."

"I'll try, but I think my arm is broken." Alaric ran a hand over his forearm, making him wince in agony.

Moving frustratingly slow, the trio buried the treasure under a towering elm tree, then hid their shovels and gear. Elle stopped short as they ambled uphill in hopes of flagging down a passerby.

"Up there," she said.

Her partners raised their eyes.

The ghastly man was waiting near the road's edge, peering down like a vengeful abomination. He raised a rotten, peeling arm. "Thieves!"

"What are you?" cried Balik, slipping to his knees as he gained no traction atop the loose leaves. The impact made him cry out in pain.

Elle glanced at Balik's commotion, then dared a second look at the stranger, but again, he had vanished. She blinked, then rubbed her tired eyes.

"What *was* that?" Alaric asked, gingerly feeling his bleeding nose. He unbuttoned his shirt to jam his arm inside, forming a makeshift sling for his purpling arm. Snorting in the blood from his nasal passages, he spit the red blob on the ground, but the act did nothing to help him breathe. It merely vibrated his nose and caused more tremendous pain.

"I don't know, but it wasn't from this world," retorted Elle. "I told you we should've left well enough alone."

"Don't be stupid," snapped Balik. "The dead can't walk and talk."

She ignored him. Facing the road again and scanning its length, she saw no further sign of the haunting figure. What she had seen filled her with mystery and reminded her of twisted tales from her youth, ones of zombies, werewolves, or other abnormal, sinister things.

If the dead could rise, might this vision seek revenge for having their deathbeds pilfered? The idea seemed absurd as it took root. *Ridiculous!* What further use could the dead possibly have for their belongings? She, on the other hand, had great use for them. The loot prevented the larcenous trio from breaking into homes and hurting people to get what they needed. The dead were long gone and could not be injured by the ransacking of their resting places. Or so she thought.

Horror raised its ugly head as the forest rumbled around them. Nightmarish spectral voices followed, echoing between the trees.

"Thieves," the dead cried in a discordant refrain.

Elle quickly realized the trio was surrounded. The repulsive circle of the dead was tightening. She scanned her surroundings. The 're-awakened,' as she hurriedly deemed them, were closing in. Certainly, it would have been easy enough to call them 'zombies,' but they were not. Zombies resulted from viruses or the like. At least they did in books and movies. These things were dead—no question of that fact.

She spun left, frantically searching for an escape route, but the way was blocked by an especially repellant dead thing. She grimaced at its appearance.

With only patches of skin holding back its intestines, the drooping innards hung down like unusually thick, pink worms. What small amount of remaining skin there was barely covered the bones as it dangled and swayed like shredded leather. White eyes peered out of its skull like large Moonstone gems, their beauty gone. She fought back a retch.

The dead thing pointed a bent, decaying finger in truthful accusation as it moaned, "Thieves," once more. Others from the right and behind wailed incomprehensibly with slacked jaws. Some held their heads at odd angles. Most dragged their feet as they came forward. But some, like the one now focused on Elle, were terrifying as they could close in with greater speed and purpose.

Elle stumbled and fell backward, landing on her palms to spider-walk as best she could. The dead thing drew close, its hands grasping and teeth gnashing. Grimacing, she lashed her foot forward to connect with its face, sending it tumbling over a slight rise. Pieces of skin and skull were left behind. Within seconds, another one took its place, its gaping maw leering for her neck or any exposed flesh it could sink its rotting teeth into. Elle continued to fight, but in her heart, she believed the end had come. The pain was excruciating as she struggled.

As her final seconds drew near, a fist-sized rock tore through her attacker's skull. Elle screamed as the head of the reawakened exploded. She scowled as the dead thing dropped across her knees, pinning her to the earth. Disgusting brain matter oozed onto her jeans.

"Bullseye," cried Balik as he limped toward her.

Elle scrambled about wildly until the thing slid onto the ground. She leapt up, winced, then grabbed Balik's hand and ran. Stabbing pain shot through her body with each step. "Thanks for saving me," she said over her shoulder. "Where's Alaric?"

Skidding to a stop, they spun to see their friend stumbling toward them. His leg was bloodied and he moved with little speed.

Elle waved him forward. "Come on! You can make it," she shouted. In a brash decision, she started to his rescue until Balik's hand halted her. He shook his head.

"Don't bother," he said.

Her objections were lost in a cry of revulsion as a flurry of movement swept over their friend. The reawakened seemed to come from nowhere as they swarmed about, bowling Alaric over, one rotting body after another attacked from every angle. Others lay prone on the ground, tangling his feet. He fell with a thud.

Kicking and punching, he cursed as they tore at him, biting and gnawing his exposed skin. Alaric's cussing hurriedly elevated to awful screams, ones lost within the thick forest as life blood poured from his ghastly wounds, staining the earthen floor red in spots.

Elle broke away from Balik, snatched up a sizeable tree branch, and charged in, swinging with all her might. She ignored her agony as the limb fell on the reawakened. She split one head, causing the dead thing to collapse at her feet. Another hew, then another, and yet another.

The swarm turned, grabbing for her like a many-limbed nightmare, but Elle stood tall, hacking away at the nearest ones. Meanwhile, Balik dragged Alaric—or what was left of him—clear. Limbs stripped to the bone, and a half-crushed skull were all that remained of their partner. He had been torn to shreds in a gruesome act of reprisal. Balik retched as he let go of the remains. Then, another piercing sound split the air.

Elle rounded to see her second partner vanish within another decaying mass of flesh and bones. There would be no saving Balik. She dropped the tree branch and fled, her traumatized mind working at a frenzied pace. Heavy, thudding footsteps followed. It sounded as if every graveyard occupant was giving chase. She glanced back. There were a dozen, with more in the distance, their grey arms flailing as they shouted again, "Thieves!"

During a moment of clarity, the answer came in a rush. Elle ran to the burial site and dropped to her knees, clawing the dirt with both hands, whimpering in pain with each movement. Grabbing the treasure, she ripped open the bags and flung the trinkets throughout the leaf-filled woods.

"Here!" she screamed. "Take your things! Take them!"

She tossed out more. More blood came in a cough. When the grunts and moans of the reawakened softened, and none grabbed for her, she staggered uphill. Looking back, she watched the dead gather round their former treasures. All but one. The man from the road. He pursued her still, hobbling upward through the leaves, his one eye unblinking.

"What do you want!" she howled as more blood soaked her chin. She spat out the red fluid. "I've nothing left."

"Thieves," came his answer as he pointed to her.

Finally, in another spot of lucidity, Elle realized she still wore the ring. Unnerved, she tugged, twisted, and pulled until it felt like her finger would snap off. Elle spit on her knuckle, watching the crimson-stained saliva run beneath the black band. She pulled again. Freedom!

"Here, damn you! Take it," she yelled. Rearing back, she flung the band as far as she could, then dropped to the ground, coughing and wheezing. She held her ribs. More blood.

The dead thing made a horrible sound, then twisted about and ambled away.

Elle scurried toward the road, half-crawling as her legs threatened to buckle with each step. After a seeming eternity, she reached the pavement, then looked down at the meandering, noisy reawakened. They still mindlessly gathered their treasures, baubles, and trinkets by the handful. It seemed the dead cared greatly about their possessions and had returned to gain them back at any cost.

Disbelief twisted Elle's sweaty face. She watched for some while, wondering if greed ever truly leaves a person, even in death. The concept was disgusting—abhorrent in many ways. Vowing never to own a piece of gold or silver again, she hobbled down the road without looking back.

Stealing was immoral in her eyes, yet it proved a way to avoid the harshness of real life. Pressing hunger for an easy living had led the trio here, but the cost had been high indeed. She never thought about the terrible outcome awaiting her if greed overtook decency. It was worse than the fear that led her to this point—fear of being stuck in the rut of working until her dying day.

Her brows crunched in disgust, knowing the reawakened were right—she and her companions had simply been thieves, taking what did not belong to them. Ultimately, all their bountiful treasure gains had been forfeited, save for a single life. Hers. And the further Elle got from the wretched sight, trailing blood in her wake, the greater her realization it was more than enough.

THE KNIFE

One suggestive thought occupied Carl's mind as his shuffling foot-steps broke the peaceful night. The notion centered on the alluring woman by his side who, mere minutes ago, vowed to relieve all his burdens. She promised to set him free from his everyday cares. They would disappear forever. The price would be steep, but he cared little for that worry.

Desire spread through his loins as he watched her walk. She was go-ing to be worth every penny. He yearned for her shapely body to serve as a channel for his sexual release. Perhaps regularly, if he could con-vince her and the fee was right. After all, his wife would never know.

Once in a shadowed corner, they embraced briefly. For a fleeting moment, the pale moon highlighted her delicate features. But the view was brief as puffy clouds returned, plunging the couple into copious darkness. Night's hold restored itself, pressing down with an unnatural invisible weight.

"You're so beautiful. And I . . . I . . . I don't even know your name. What do I call you?" stammered Carl.

"Does it matter?" She shoved his large frame hard against the stone wall.

Her strength surprised him, causing fantasies to dance in his mind as his pink tongue ran over both lips. He clutched her breasts and smiled. "Like it rough, do ya? I'm going to enjoy this." Seizing her hips, he pulled her close to spread wet kisses on her neck.

In that instant, pain ripped through his body. The sensation was more than a wasp sting, yet not as bad as losing a finger, as he had done years ago in a butcher shop accident.

Words would not form. Carl only mustered a snort reminiscent of a rotund hog snuffling its food. Bewildered, his thoughts evaporated into confusion. Turning his stare downward, he spotted a wooden hilt protruding from his muscular torso. His hand hovered over the handle for a long instant as he stood, conflicted with what to do.

The extent of his error finally reached his brain as dampness spread across his stomach and down his legs. The blade had passed between bone and through soft flesh. Another snort escaped before several mumbled words spilled out in a feeble plea for help. Even now, the uncaring breeze carried his orations far into the night, unheard by any other living soul except his murderer and a pair of cats watching the scene unfold from atop a trashcan.

Nearing the chilly edges of death, Carl tipped forward, his eyes rolling back before his body met the pavement with a grotesque slap. It was over. He moved no more. Blood pooled around his frame as his soul tumbled deeper into a dismal, murkier world from which there was no return.

Night's obscurity welcomed the woman as she stared at the body like a lover. "It's Bonnie," she said. "My name is Bonnie. Not that you'll ever know it." She rolled the big man over, retrieved her knife, then wiped it clean on his trousers as a final insult.

At that moment, a man's voice, one only the woman heard, rose. It was relentless in its twisted desires. 'Death, sweet death. Well done! Give me more!'

"Shut up! No more! I've had enough!" she screamed into the darkness. She bit her lip until blood flowed, resisting the uninvited words with all her strength. She spun to leave as the voice called again.

'I will set you free very soon. Just one more. Kill!'

She spasmed to resist. "Promise me I'll be free after the next one. I want this over with."

'You have my word. I will leave your life forever.'

Bonnie sighed with resignation. The inner torment stopped as she moved toward the light, lost in thought. In days past, Bonnie had tried reasoning with the horrible piece of evil but failed each attempt. She had already killed so many. This was the first time the blade had promised to release her.

She pondered if the whispering echoes were genuine or merely a skilled deception. If true, Bonnie could not wait for the day. She was entirely aware of her mistake to give the cruel thing the death it craved, but in her mind, what choice did she have? Still, killing a random, innocent person to keep her sanity felt wrong. Perverted and sick. Yet she would be free. That was all that mattered as she stepped from the shadows like a victorious soldier emerging from battle.

The odious voice vanished once her foot touched the faintly lit street. Bonnie straightened her long green coat, then fashioned her flowing hair into a ponytail. She smiled as the evening bus rounded the corner.

After glancing at her watch, she moved to the sheltered stop, hoping the ordeal would end. "Right on time."

'We're nearly done. But the night is young, and there is death to do. Just one more.'

"Leave me be, damn you! I've done what you asked! That's enough for tonight." Mouthing a silent scream, she clapped both hands over her ears to keep the words from probing the inner depths of her mind.

As the air brakes hissed, the red, double-decker bus rolled to a stop. To Bonnie's relief, the noise smothered out the repulsive voice, forcing the intruder from her head again. The doors swung wide, and after another jerky spasm, she smiled thinly at the driver as she boarded.

"Good evening, miss," he offered happily.

Bonnie displayed a strained smile as she lowered onto the empty bench seat directly behind the rotund man.

A second loud hiss rang out before the bus moved on. "Off we go. Movin' on," the driver announced.

With a measured glance over her shoulder, Bonnie noted twenty passengers. Both eyes moved forward again as she hoped to arrive home before the voice returned. But no sooner had a city block passed before the torment returned. 'Do it now! No one will stop you. Kill them all.'

Squeezing her eyes shut, Bonnie gripped the seatback. "Shut up, you bastard! You said just one! Keep your filthy mouth closed."

The unsuspecting passengers jumped at her outburst. Some mumbled disapproval but dared not confront her with a direct complaint. Others shrugged the incident off, paying her no more attention.

But again, Bonnie's voice raced down the aisle as another curse-filled outburst spewed from her lips. All eyes focused on her as eerie silence spread over the passengers like a plague. Several folks took up different seats in the back. Others shifted uneasily, and more than a few glanced longingly out into the night as if attempting to block her from their thoughts.

A third shudder ripped through Bonnie as the steady sound of the throbbing diesel engine grew overwhelming. To the good, its horrible rhythmic pulse kept the voice at bay.

"Ma'am, are you okay? Should I pull over?" asked the driver, glancing in the overhead mirror. His former pleasant smile was replaced with concern. "You don't look so good."

"Neither do you," snarled Bonnie. She sprang forward, grabbed a handful of his thick hair, then hauled herself upright with a swift movement. Jerking his head back, she slid the sharp steel across his throat. Behind her, the passengers screamed and cowered, frozen in their seats.

The voice returned with a satisfied sigh. 'Excellent! Well done, my love. You will be free soon.'

Bright red bubbles gurgled from the driver's gaping wound. His palms smacked his flesh as pudgy fingers groped and squeezed at the slit, trying to staunch the fatal bleeding. Another chorus of screams rose from the back.

The fellow shuddered, then expired to slump over the wheel. The bus veered from the roadway, swaying left and right before impacting a building corner.

The motorized metal beast careened from a shop loading ramp, angling it onto two wheels. Skidding back into the street, it threw dazed passengers beneath its weight. Many fell from the open upper level and through lower windows to roll over the pavement like marbles. Several scrambled toward safety, but none got far before the massive machine tipped over, crushing them beneath its bulk as it landed. Their shouts of terror fell short as their bodies transformed into smeared crimson trails on the roadway.

Others were tossed about like an angry child's discarded playthings, dying in twisted, broken positions, stuffed beneath seats, or smothered under the pile of ruined bodies.

'Death! Sweet death! Watch them die! Kill them all!'

Bonnie's leather coat offered little protection as she catapulted through the broken windshield to glance off several parked cars, landing with a thump on the blacktop. The resounding snap of her neck rose above all else. The knife flung from her lifeless hand to skitter away with a ringing sound. The blade fell unnoticed in a shop doorway, gleaming dully beneath a soft overhead light.

Within moments, the ghastly accident attracted a mass of gawking onlookers, but only one heard the hypnotic voice. A woman's light, sensual tone filled his ears.

As the insect-like murmuring of the crowd grew, and sirens wailed in the distance, a well-dressed fellow peered around, paying little attention to the carnage. Puzzled, he strode casually along in search of the voice as his eyes searched through the dim streetlight.

"Where's that comin' from?" he muttered. His gaze flicked up to touch the various faces, studying them with interest, yet he frowned at each. Removing his hat, he scratched his head and whispered, "I hear you, my precious one. Where are you?"

Pacing the street, his eyes back to the ground, he reached a splintered, shabby doorway, halting to stare at the silver blade before claiming it as his own. He wiped it clean with a kerchief.

"There you are, my love. I heard ya' callin'. That's a mighty temptin' sound ya' be singin' tonight." His smile widened as he stroked the hilt with growing adoration. Running a thumb sideways over the blade's edge, he gave an approving whistle. "My, yur sharp, missy."

Nodding agreement as the beautiful voice spoke in his mind, he answered. "Yes, my darlin', we have work to do. And a lot of it, I would say." He tucked his treasure away and strode past the throng, paying them no more mind. "By the way, me name is Jack. I'm sure we'll be gettin' along splendidly, we will."

'You have such strong hands, Jack. I love that in a man. My name is Bonnie. I promise to be yours until the very end.'

DREAMS

Journal entry: Oct. 15, 1882.

Dreams are harmless in most respects. Complex hallucinations of the mind, according to the learned scientific community. While their purpose remains unknown and the subject of much debate, I assure you they are not always benevolent. But that is no surprise to any who venture, willingly or not, into the dream realm.

Consider the archetype of falling endlessly, building anticipation as you plummet through time and space to land abruptly in death or, more distressingly, never at all. The mere thought of an unexpected ending causes one's heart to flutter until it can stand no more and hastily stops all pulsations.

Perhaps you dream of colorful rainbows, happy places, puppies, kittens, or unicorns. How I wish I could join you in these cheerful places. For my visions are, in totality, vexing. In the terrible night, the demise of each day brings, horrible outcomes await me. On some occasions, I am relentlessly persecuted by nasty things that bite, pinch, and gnaw every inch of my person. These unnamed creatures and twisted beasts

subjugate me, tearing at my flesh unmercifully. More often, a lone tor-
turer dispenses punishment for unspoken offenses I have no recollec-
tion of committing. His maltreatment carries the most dread. In each
case, my sole thought is a speedy end. I welcome death rather than this
unfavorable reiteration of agonizing pain.

For reasons beyond my comprehension, sleep is a chamber of hor-
rors from which I have no reprieve. I have tried to do without rest, to
remove it from my life. Yet, lacking respite, my mortal body will falter
and cease to exist. It is cruelty beyond words knowing my most dreaded fear is the very thing that maintains both sanity and health.

I beg you to harken my tale, for these may be my final thoughts
before I am hurriedly taken to my expiry. Even as I pen these words,
I wonder if any shall ever discover them. I hope to save unsuspecting
souls from a nightmarish existence similar, or worse, if possible, than
what I currently suffer.

I fight with what waning strength I have left to disallow my eyelids
from growing heavy and closing, for it may be forevermore. Should I
be unable to save myself from this fiendish reverie, know my journey
was most unkind. My ending days began not long ago, quite innocently. Before fading, I will attempt to transcribe the events as I recall them.
For the record, my name is Sir Theodore Marsh II.

––––––––––

Our small gathering began innocuously enough. Present were no more
than five of my fellows gathered for a night of mystery and frightening
intrigue. As was our habit, we started by reading tales of suspense, murder, mayhem, and evil spirits—wonderous compositions of the written
word from many whose imaginations far outreached my own. Here,
I hasten to make a point: my affliction does not come from the inner
depths of my mind nor from the stories recited at such gatherings. The
events I speak of are genuine and unasked for, I assure you.

Since I do not partake in alcohol or narcotics, as they greatly dull one's wits, when speaking of my problem, I am revealing only the truth despite the subject causing me personal embarrassment. How the visions began, I cannot tell. Perhaps I unknowingly opened an evil gateway into my mind by completing a haunted story or uttering a lone word during an earlier reading on a different day. To my dismay, I may never know the answer.

As Corthina, my ex-lover, read on the evening in question, one story captivated my intellect and drew me in as her words leapt from the pages. It concerned vengeful, wicked spirits who, with little effort, harmed or plagued you during hours of slumber. This was indeed close to my own memories.

Once our meeting concluded, I strolled home, enjoying the cool spring air against my skin. The moon rode high, and stars littered the sky, shining down with their wondrous light as I pondered the tale my former partner recited. The words, from Lord Chadwick Challandon, a foremost expert—if there can be such a person concerning this lurid subject—named the phobia, T.B.D., meaning, 'tormented by dreams.' His conclusions sounded entirely accurate.

I have often asked myself how one could defeat a demon, spirit, or being, particularly one that cannot be touched or conversed with to any point of logic. But my depth of the subject's knowledge is far shallower than I care to admit.

In my situation, terror rises at night from being bruised, beaten, slashed, eaten, hacked, or dismembered. I wake with fresh scars upon my body where the unnatural assault occurred. Disturbingly, the situation is a paradox as my injuries heal and vanish by day's end in preparation to repeat the torment anew with each nightfall. Hence, my harrowing, inescapable cycle.

Usually, my tormentor wears a mask or hood, but on rare occasions, I catch fleeting glimpses of a leering face moments before he dons the covering. Man-like in many respects, yet beastly in others, he exudes pure evil, taking unparalleled delight in my excruciating pain, shrill screams, and bottomless fear, that much I know. As well, the brute relishes my helplessness during my dream state. Would he stop if asked? I am inclined to think not.

My last episode of torment saw me facing upward, miserably strapped to a torture rack of fiendish design. I tried to ascertain what terrible circumstances would befall me this evening but could not say. Beheaded? Torn apart? Buried alive? Eaten alive by the nameless creatures existing only in this place? Certainly not, as all those atrocious harms had already befallen my body in different dreams. I am confident that tonight will be something unfamiliar, as the tortures always were. Perhaps they would be even more wicked than previous versions.

I concentrated on my present dilemma once the feel of hardwood beneath my pliable, naked skin grew stronger. Unnerved, I squirmed to test my bonds—a pointless effort. My gaze roved over my body to reveal my only article of clothing to be a dirty loincloth. I trembled from a cold beyond any bitter temperature I could recall.

With another look, I noted my prison seemed rectangular, with strange niches and disfigured walls. Small, dark shapes skittered here and there in the shadows, their claws tapping stone as they quickly hid themselves from my gaze. Unseen or not, they caused my heart to race. Would they be the instruments of my demise tonight?

As the web of perpetual dreams lowered me deeper into another unraveling hallucination, a faint noise resounded in my consciousness, much like water from a leaking faucet or perhaps blood falling upon an unfeeling stone floor.

Scanning again, I discerned my left hand's third and fourth fingers were missing, cut cleanly away. The sound was my blood trickling from the rack's edge with a constant drip onto the black masonry below.

Rattled, my voice raised an octave as I cried for mercy. But I found none that night, nor any other, for that matter. My limbs shook from fear with potent effect. Had the opportunity to escape presented itself,

I doubt, with any degree of seriousness, I would have prevailed in taking advantage of it. Now, sanity blurred even more.

Then, my hooded persecutor appeared, seemingly at his whim, for I heard no door open, secret passage reveal itself, or chair grate the ground from where he once sat. He simply appeared as if wished into existence by supernatural powers contained in his mind.

Lumbering to my side, he hurriedly loosened the biting ropes binding my ankles and wrists. I was crudely dragged from my torture device only to be thrust against a cold, rough wall. The impactful force knocked the wind from my lungs. Blood from my missing digits splattered the wall with a sickening, viscous sound. I closed my eyes to the sight and turned away.

My breath came in raspy gasps. Tears wet my eyes as both hands were jerked high above my head, anchored tightly with iron manacles that cut into my flesh. My strength to resist was at a low. I am sure greater punishment would have befallen me if I had tried. As was becoming customary, I endured the glaring pain.

After resecuring my limp body, my tormentor backed away, glaring. Laughing hideously, he raised a muscular arm, drew it back, then lashed at my soft, weak tissue with a cruel whip, shredding pieces from my figure despite my weakening pleas for mercy. My petitions only brought forth harder, faster lashes. The agony was, as one can imagine, insufferable. I went silent, refusing to show my demoralizing suffering any longer, knowing the former lent speed to the creature during my foul treatment.

Finally, a respite. I had little idea how many lashes my body bore, yet by the telltale signs of my filleted skin, perhaps fifty or more. Deceived in the respect my suffering was singular, I fathomed at that moment others were enduring the same cruelties. This part was new. Never had strangers appeared in my room of anguish.

To my left hung a woman, her arms secured much like my own. Both legs were bent at odd angles. Her breasts were slashed and bleeding. Her left ear was missing. She moaned an agonized noise but produced no intelligible sounds. Still, as she found the drive to look into my eyes with her remaining strength, I understood what my own sad visage must seem like, though to a much lesser extent, I believe. Could her broken form be a sickening mirror of what would come my way? I convulsed involuntarily and counted my blessings, convinced this senseless monster was not through with either of us.

On my right hung partially fleshed remnants of rotting skeletons. While bones, attached to their owners or not, are not scary to most, the odor from their decaying flesh wormed its way into my nostrils—a smell I will remember until my death. Which, in my current state, may take me soon.

Indeed, the rats feasting on the corpses were pleased. Perhaps someday, they would clean my bones, too. Across the room lay human remnants piled high in a crooked corner. Their height soared to a tall man's head with a width of some fifteen feet. The depth I could only guess since its edge vanished into a deep shadow.

Ahead, a man's body hung inverted, his feet wrapped in strong chains as he swayed like a human pendulum, keeping abnormal time in this disgusting place. His arms were missing, and the wounds were cauterized to prevent blood loss and prolong suffering. He was alive in some fashion, his eyes searching the room as I had. Like the broken woman, dreadful noises issued from his mouth as he attempted to communicate.

It took long moments for me to realize his tongue had been removed. The sickening, fleshy trophy was nailed to a thick wooden post beside him.

I openly wept, not only for the others but for myself, as well. Two questions slogged through my mind. What madness keeps me here? How did I, a man of fine standing, intelligence, and hard work, fall prey to this insufferable loop of anguish and wrongdoings? Being neither a wizard nor a god, I could not end the atrocities around me, no matter how much I plied my will to make it so. Then, as quickly as the awful vision had begun, it ended.

———————

As I woke, my gaze hurried straight to my fingers, which, as before, had thankfully been restored, completely intact. Further inspection noted my body was mostly unaffected from the lashings, save the revolting scars still lining my face, limbs, and torso. Those would fade by day's end, I thought. At least they had before as I woke from each previous bitter dream.

Considering my conundrum, I have discovered a remarkably unclear line between reality and madness. Many nights, as I refused to sleep, my tormentor seemed mere inches away, pulling me into the void of dreams he alone ruled. Initially, he would never venture close enough to place his hands upon me in waking hours. But nothing ever remains the same.

Now, even with my eyes wide open, I feel his presence, a hot breath in my ear, a mighty hand upon my shoulder, an irresistible creeping sensation. This abomination knows no matter the cost or outcome, I must sleep. He uses that knowledge to mock me in sunlight—another torment.

Then, in a twisted, awful epiphany, I wondered if I had ever genuinely felt the sun upon my face, tasted a woman's kiss, or witnessed beautiful sunrises. Or, has my entire life been there, trapped in the depths of his depravity, unable to escape? Perhaps my host simply allows me to experience these things to give me hope—hope to stay alive one more day while wishing for freedom. This concept is boundless in its perverse application.

I say freedom of any kind is an unattainable illusion, a breath of fresh air I shall never discover. Undoubtedly, I am trapped. My life, as I had known it, seems to be little more than falsehood.

As revealed earlier, I leave this memoir, such as it is, to any who may find it. Providing others besides myself even exist. Or are they dreams, too, like my detailing of these events? I may never know, for these all-too-potent nightmares rule my existence.

Have I slipped into madness? For I no longer distinguish between wakeful hours or sleep—held prisoner in an evil realm that, in some fashion or another, controls my conscious mind, diluting my will and leading me astray in all actions.

In this, my final urgent plea to you, the reader, harken my tale before I fade forever as darkness slowly descends again.

I have reached the regrettable conclusion that dreams are hidden traps. Some merely disguise themselves as happy images. Yet, wrapped inside each is absolute danger, begging you to open your mind to their evil. If you glean no other piece of wisdom from my plight, heed these words, lest you also become trapped: Never dream.

POTION MASTER

As Marv slid across the vinyl bus seat, he hoped today would be different. But it never was. The moment he entered the belly of the beast and the doors closed, he was trapped.

"Hey, dopey, what did you bring me for lunch?" Kevin, two years older and a foot taller than Marv, hung over the back of his seat. "Hand it over, loser."

Five pairs of eyes turned toward them. Marv wished he could be invisible.

James, a linebacker on the football team, hopped across the aisle to squish Marv up against the cold, metal wall. "Yeah, what's for lunch today, dork? Did mommy make you PB&J sandwiches with the crusts cut off again?"

"Damn it! How many times do I have to tell you I hate PB&J? They're for babies." Kevin reached a thick arm out to smack Marv's head, driving his cranium against the window with a loud crack.

Marv grimaced. So far, the Enemy, as he thought of the tormenting group of six, had not done anything worse than he had seen before.

They would punch him, flick his ears, destroy his homework, or shove him around like he was a pinball machine. They were not the most creative, but their methods instilled fear. And a significant degree of hate.

"I'm tired of waiting. Gimme your lunch." James elbowed Marv in the ribs so hard it knocked the air from the helpless boy's lungs.

Marv gasped, shame burning in him after realizing his eyes were wet. That feeling evaporated into anger as he dreamed of telling James off or retaliating in some fashion. Unfortunately, he wasn't brave enough to stand up to any of the gang. Except for Tracy, they were all nearly twice his size. Yet, he hated James and Kevin the most. They were the worst. Whenever one of them breathed their foul, nicotine-laden breath on him or gave him a whack, he wished they would die. If only someone would bully the bullies.

Feeling he had no choice, Marv revealed the lunch bag his mom had packed and meekly offered it to James, who opened it and then divided the loot among the rest of the gang. Kevin took the pudding cup. Tracy received the apple since she was on a perpetual diet. James stuck the sandwich in his own backpack. Todd, Marsha, and Sarah split the package of Twizzlers.

Marv should have hidden it in the bottom of his backpack. After all, he went through the trouble of sneaking it from the snack cupboard.

At least now, after the Enemy had tormented him to their satisfaction, they left him alone until they reached school. There, he waited until everyone was off the bus before making his way down the empty aisle. At least no one was there to trip him this time. He quickly hopped over a puddle and shuffled up the sidewalk toward the front doors. A gaggle of classmates passed him, jabbering away, then laughing as someone shoved him into a different puddle beside the sidewalk. Marv closed his eyes to the scornful looks as the cold, muddy water soaked his skin.

Wet and miserable, he resigned himself to be a target for the rest of his high school career. He didn't even bother going to the washroom to clean up. It felt pointless since someone was likely waiting for him there, too.

That night in his room, he crawled into bed, wrapped himself in the blankets, and cried. Thoughts of bringing his dad's gun or a sharp knife to school danced in his head. He doubted he would ever have the courage to do anything so rash, let alone to use either one. Confrontation was not his style. He could only wait for the day the Neanderthals graduated or flunked out of high school.

———

"This *rat*," seethed James, grabbing a fistful of Marv's shirt and cocking back his other hand, "put rotten meat in the sandwich! You could have killed me, you—"

The bus doors swished open at that moment, making everyone's heads turn. Marv took advantage and yanked himself out of James's grip. He pushed himself further into his seat while craning his neck to see past his outsized peers. A new student had boarded. The boy, who looked older than the others, wore chinos and a dress shirt instead of jeans and a t-shirt. He walked calmly through the crowded bus to lower himself beside the bullied young man.

"What the hell?" James muttered, taking a step back. His curled first dropped.

Kevin gave Marv a shot to the back of the head anyway. "What did you do, pay this guy to sit next to you? What a loser."

Fit, clean-cut, and fashionable, the new boy turned to Marv and asked, "These guys bothering you?"

Marv gave a slight nod to the floor. "It's no big deal," he lied.

A thick, powerful-looking hand extended. "I'm Seth."

Marv was surprised. Not many kids spoke to him, and if they did, it was mean. This small gesture made him like the new guy straightaway. He shook Seth's hand. "Marv."

"Marv, the perv," Kevin said. "And Seth the—"

"Do you mind?" Seth turned in his seat to interrupt, narrowing his eyes at the bully. "It's past time for you to shut up and sit down. Do it now."

Kevin, too stunned for words, slid down in his seat, silent. Marv hid his grin behind one hand. He savored the small victory yet felt his smile faltering. Despite the warm greeting, Marv expected Seth to hang out with the cool crowd once he settled in. As the bus lurched forward again, he sat back and carefully side-eyed his seatmate.

Despite his preppy appearance, Seth's presence felt akin to a jock who would be more at home on a football field than hanging out with a loser like him. Marv thought the new kid would likely learn the ropes by the end of the day and pick on him, just like everyone else.

Turned out he was wrong.

As the week wore on, every form of bullying stopped whenever Seth boarded the bus. Clearly, the other kids were afraid of him. Were they afraid he would tell on them, or worse? Marv did not have the faintest idea but was grateful, nonetheless.

Just as he became comfortable with the peace, Seth was absent on one Friday. Things abruptly reverted to normal—punching, name-calling, and lunch stealing. When Seth returned on Monday, he knew everything that had happened while he was gone, not that it was difficult to discern. Marv's black eye was a blatant giveaway.

As September shifted into October, Seth invited Marv to hang out at his house one day after school. "My parents are out of town for the weekend, and I wouldn't mind the company."

"Cool," Marv said, "but I have to be home for dinner. Mom's making my favorite meatloaf."

"Sure, dude. No problem." Seth unlocked the front door as Marv texted his mom.

Rather than showing him around the house, Seth led him up the broad stairs toward his bedroom. Marv innocently trailed his finger along the banister, noting it was clean, just like his new friend always seemed to be. In fact, from the glimpse he had gotten as they went, the house looked spotless.

As the door swung wide, Marv gasped. "Whoa. This is cool." He felt like he'd entered another realm. "This is your bedroom! Man, you really love Halloween."

Seth dropped his backpack on the black satin comforter covering the large bed. "Sure, I dig it. Feel free to look around. Just don't touch anything. I'm not responsible if you turn yourself into an ogre or worse."

"Ha! Good one," said Marv, pausing in front of an intricately carved cabinet securing cauldrons of various sizes. Next came several rows of neatly organized bottles filled with shimmering liquids of all colors that moved as if alive. "Wow. Those are cool. Hey, what are the knives for?"

"Those are called athames—pronounced ath-a-may. They're used during spell crafting." Seth retrieved one to hand it over. The others lay on the black velvet altar cloth covering the desktop. Around them were various statues of ancient gods.

"That's Anubis, Guide to the Underworld." Marv touched the ones he recognized. "Ganesh, Remover of Obstacles. Shiva, the Destroyer. Hades, King of the Underworld. Morrigan, The Great Queen."

"Who is also known as The Phantom Queen," added Seth.

"Right. You seem to have a dark theme going here."

"I'm impressed you know so much about them. Well done."

Marv shrugged as he blushed from the compliment. "Most days, the library is the safest place to hide."

His eyes continued to rove. Around him stood candles of all sizes, shapes, and colors on every surface. Marv knew his mother would have a fit if he ever lit one candle in his room, let alone dozens. Brilliantly colored lava lamps bubbled on shelves along the far wall. Blacklight posters were hung on nearly every open space. Marv ran his fingers over them, loving the feel of the velvety material.

"Did you see these?" Seth pointed to a narrow glass case. Inside were several pieces of Pagan jewelry—necklaces, rings, and bracelets—portraying triple moons, images of ravens, Celtic knots, and more. Each article appeared old and valuable, unlike the junky stuff in the mall.

Marv sighed as he turned a full circle to take it all in. *How cool would it be to have a room like this? To live here with Seth as a brother? I would feel safe all the time.*

Seth patted the bed next to him. "Sit. I'll teach you some of the things I like to do."

"Um . . . I . . ." Marv was stopped by his pocket vibrating. He frowned. "Crap. That'll be my mom."

"Tell her you're staying here for dinner." Seth leaned back on his hands and seemed almost amused.

Marv's confidence suddenly wavered. He was not used to people being nice to him, and he was unsure how to act. Embarrassed after taking his call, he held up his phone. "It's meatloaf night. I'd better go."

"Suit yourself," Seth said. "But if you want to get back at the bullies for what they're doing, let me know. The veil is thinnest in October. It's the best time to work a little magic."

Marv, unsure of what his new friend was talking about, laughed awkwardly and left.

———

Magic wasn't real. Marv knew that, or at least thought he did. But within a week, after his friend's words had played in his head each day and James had given him another black eye in the locker room, Marv returned to Seth's house, itching to talk about magic and the paranormal.

"My friend, I know just what you need." Seth went to the cabinet for a vial holding swirling green mist, then handed it over. "This will help."

Marv stared as the mist undulated like a caged beast. "Help with what?"

"Your bully problem, of course." His friend chuckled. "Have you been paying attention?"

Marv's ears grew warm. "What good is this? Am I supposed to throw it at them?"

Seth chuckled again as he gathered items around the room—a small cauldron, one black chime candle, matches, a bottle of oil, and some herbs. After setting them on a sturdy table, he lit several more candles, lowered the shades, and closed the curtains. Then he turned to add a few carefully selected herbs to the cauldron.

"Are you casting a spell?" Marv asked.

"Nope. *We* are. And it's so simple it's almost painful," Seth said as he lit the chime candle. "What you're holding is a Wish Potion. Sort of like Aladdin's lamp. You make a wish, pour the contents in the cauldron, and say a few magical words." He clapped his hands together twice. "Then, voila, you're done."

"What's it all for?"

"Let's just say you'll be able to solve your own problems after this."

Marv frowned. "What do you mean?"

"You, my friend, will have the power to become whatever your mind can create. Personally, I prefer monsters merely for the terror factor. Kevin, James, and their friends have tormented you for years. Isn't it time they got a taste of what they've been dishing out?"

Marv's heart raced. For the first time since they met, he had the sneaking suspicion his new friend could be nuttier than he realized. Right now, he did not care. "How would I do that?"

"By using this spell." Seth grinned. "And by letting me teach you everything I know."

"But you're just a kid. Like me."

Seth touched Marv's cheek. His fingertips were like ice, making Marv bit his lip from the rush of coolness.

"I'm so much more. Think of it!" The older boy swept an arm around the room. "This could all be yours. All you must do is learn how to recreate each potion and spell."

Marv gazed at the books and potions lining the shelves, then toward the door. "That'll take years. Why would you do this for me? I mean, it's totally cool, but . . ."

"Because we're friends." Seth grinned again, his face twisting in the candlelight.

"You're not really a kid, are you?" Marv asked slowly, his heart thumping in wait for the answer. "How long have you been doing this?"

Youthfulness seemed to fade from Seth's face as lines burrowed into his skin. "I've been alive for a long time and have seen a great deal." The lines smoothed out as the candlelight flickered. "I've never had to recruit an apprentice before, though."

Marv tried not to flinch at what he'd seen or what he thought he'd seen. Perhaps it was a trick of the light. Either way, it could not explain his pounding heartbeat. Had he inadvertently sold his soul by stepping into Seth's inner sanctum? He thought it was the way things like this happened in movies. "An apprentice to carry on your work, you mean?"

"Exactly."

"Why me?" he asked sheepishly.

Seth toyed with one of the candles. "You and I have a problem we can solve if we work together. You can become whatever you want to rid yourself of these bullies. I can teach you how."

Marv pondered the words. He didn't want to *become* anything. He simply wanted the bullying to end. "Why would anyone want to become a monster? That means I'd be just like them."

"Slow down, my friend. You want the bullies to leave you alone, and I simply wish to pass along my knowledge."

"What kind of knowledge? Witchcraft?" questioned Marv.

"Mostly." Seth held up a hand. "However, understand there are drawbacks."

"Like what?" Not sure what else to do, Marv opened his backpack to grab the pack of Twizzlers he'd hidden beneath his gym shorts for school. He ripped it open and offered one to Seth, who bit off an end and chewed it slowly.

"Your life will change in many ways. Do you think you can handle it?"

Marv considered saying no but decided against possibly shutting his friend's enthusiasm down. "If it stops the bullies, yeah."

"Good, because that's the most important part. You could become a superhero to others who are picked on. That's where the changing part comes in." Seth placed his hands on Marv's shoulders. "Personally, I've been a werewolf, vampire, gargoyle, and many other creatures, depending on the situation. There are thousands of potion combinations. With your sharp mind, you're perfect for the task." His eyes narrowed. "You don't look convinced. You *do* want to stop the bullies, right?"

Marv nodded but was skeptical. "Yes, but . . . none of those creatures you mentioned are real. They are myths. Fairytales."

"Of course they're real. And all you need to do is make the wish." He guided Marv toward the cauldron. "We'll do a practice run before casting the final spell."

Marv broke out in a sweat. Everything was moving too fast but backing out seemed impossible now. Again, he didn't want to upset his friend. "Okay."

"Perfect," Seth whispered. "First, make your wish. Then, say these words. Repeat after me." He closed his eyes, raised his hands high, and turned his eyes upward as he chanted in a deep voice, one more commanding than Marv had ever heard him use.

Ancient gods
Hear my plea
Cast thy charms
Unto me
Bestow in shade
Thine hallowed form
So shall it be
Forevermore."

Seth finished. "Now it's your turn. Make your wish, then follow along."

Swallowing hard, Marv made his wish and then echoed Seth's words while keeping one eye open. He expected the room to shake, a ghostly apparition to appear, or some form of mystical, ancient powers to manifest before them.

Nothing happened.

"Pour the potion into the cauldron," Seth whispered.

Marv emptied the vial as told. Awe took him as the green mist transformed into a deep red smoke rose, swirling the scent of cinnamon throughout the room. His favorite smell.

"That's amazing." He leaned over the cauldron and drew in a deep breath. The sweet scent was akin to a foreign power entering his body, giving him mental clarity and courage. His shoulders eased back as he relaxed.

Then, before he could take another breath, his stomach tightened and twisted hard. He doubled over as pain wracked his body. Thankfully, it only lasted a handful of seconds.

"You didn't tell me about that. Did I do something wrong?" Marv straightened slowly, rubbing his stomach.

Seth shrugged. "Not at all. It's an unfortunate side effect of the process. You may have a bit of pain each time, but it grows less with every spell. Did you make your wish?"

Marv nodded. "Yep. Now what?"

"Now you go home and get some sleep."

"That's it?"

Seth leaned over the cauldron and breathed deeply. His eyes took on a bloodred glow. "Spells take time, little dude. We'll see what comes of it tomorrow."

———————

The car swerved from the road to avoid the monster. James screamed as his sweaty palms steered hard right. Despite his quick reactions, he could not stop the vehicle from plunging over the embankment.

The monster followed quickly, arriving seconds later to rip free a large tree branch and plunge it repeatedly through the convertible's roof. More screams filled the air as several voices cried, begging to be spared. Their ignored pleas were soon silenced as blood rose in high trails of crimson death with each thrust.

The monster threw the branch aside to lift the car high, shaking it like a tambourine. After several stout waggles, it stopped to sniff. Satisfied the humans were dead, he tossed the bloodied metal shell onto the ground. Seizing the limb again, it stabbed the branch through the roof a final time before roaring, then lumbering into the night.

Marv awoke in a sweat. He ran into his bathroom to splash cold water on his face before vomiting. Staring at his reflection, he assured himself it was only a dream. A nightmare. Then he saw the scratch that ran across his cheek. When did that happen?

He glanced at his fingernails, relieved to see blood beneath the sharp corner of one. He must have clawed his face during the dream. Yes, indeed, that was all. Once his heart rate slowed, he returned to bed and scooted under the covers. Something jabbed his arm. With a scowl, he swiped several small pieces of bark from between his sheets and onto the floor, then froze.

Bile rose in his throat. It *was* a dream, wasn't it?

———

Saturday morning dawned bright with thick, puffy clouds dotting the sky. Marv woke late and trundled downstairs to find his parents gone. A letter on the counter told him they were out for an early hike around Potter's Lake. He was glad for that. As he set to work making his breakfast, ruminating on the confusing dream, Seth knocked on the front door.

"Bro! Come on in. What's new?" Marv led him to the kitchen.

"Depends. How was your night?" Seth asked, raising an eyebrow.

Marv pushed aside the dream and all thoughts of tree bark as he set the table. "Good. Pretty average, I guess."

"I found something to make you feel better. Check it out." Seth placed his iPhone on the table and tapped it once.

Marv slid some eggs onto a plate and handed it to Seth, along with a tall glass of juice and two pieces of jam-covered toast. Then he served up his own breakfast, and he sat to check Seth's phone.

"How did you get on Tracy's Facebook page? What the . . . ?"

Seth chuckled. "I simply read her posts." His eyes slid down her entry, timestamped an hour ago: 'I can't believe they're gone! James, Marsha, Sarah, and Todd died in an accident on Old Sutter Road, out near Potter's Lake. W.T.F.! I'm shocked.'

Marv threw a quick glance at Seth before continuing.

'Police say James was speeding and missed the turn. No one will say more than that. My heart is broken.'

"Shit, does she really need four broken heart emojis? We get it already," grumbled Marv. The entry contained several more, too—primarily sad faces and ones looking like they would vomit.

Seth flashed a wicked smile. "Seems like some of your problems are solved."

Marv's mouth dropped open. He took another glance at the list of names. "Shit! They're all bullies from the bus."

"You don't say." Seth stabbed one of his eggs, letting the yolk leak across his plate. He sopped it up with toast.

His appetite suddenly gone, Marv fought a burgeoning headache while his friend cleaned his plate. "I dreamed about this happening last night. Like a premonition or something. Only I . . . I saw a huge monster killing them all. Actually, I dreamed *I* was the monster." The edge of the table blurred. "Sorry. I'm just st . . . st . . . stunned."

"Stunned?" Seth asked, wiping his face with a napkin. "My man, be happy. Your troubles have shrunk by four, and I guarantee the other two will no longer care that you exist."

Marv clung to the solidness of the words, but his stomach remained queasy. "I hated them, for sure, but I didn't want them to die. Especially like that." He returned the phone and pointed to it. "But you're right. At least the bullying will stop."

"Thanks to you," his friend said, pointing his fork at him. "You should take greater pride in your achievements."

"What?" Marv gripped the table with unsteady hands. "I had nothing to do with it."

Seth set his fork across the middle of his plate, the tines aimed at Marv. "Not entirely true, is it? You wanted them dead, and you are most certainly involved after we cast that spell. Face it."

"Wait, hold on there," Marv stuttered. "I . . . I most certainly was not."

"Just accept it," Seth said. "Besides, it's not like your world has lost people of value."

Marv narrowed his eyes. "What do you mean, my world? You're part of it, too."

"A slip of the tongue." Seth shrugged, yet the corner of his mouth raised in a thin smile. "How does it feel to be rid of them? That's what you wished for, right?"

Sheepishly, Marv nodded as he toyed with his fork. "Y . . . y . . . yes."

"Congrats! Great job, then. Who's next?"

The world spun around Marv as he reeled. "Why the hell would you even ask that?"

Seth grinned bigger this time as he reached for his last piece of toast. He spread strawberry jelly on the surface. "You're smart, figure it out. You cast the spell and asked for things to change, and they have . . . in a big way."

"That's impossible. There's no way our spell killed four people." Throat tightening, he paused to stare out the window and gather his thoughts. "Did it?"

"The chances of it being a coincidence seem too far-fetched," offered Seth.

Marv wasn't sure, but a terrible thought came to mind. He dashed upstairs to pick the pieces of bark off his floor, then hurried back down, taking the steps two at a time. When he returned, he pushed his open palm in front of Seth. "Explain this."

Seth clapped in delight. "A tree giant? Bravo. Excellent choice. I bet an angry one, too! Ha! You *are* a sharp lad. Never forget, those people made themselves feel big by hurting others. The spell you made was much larger. Good riddance, I say."

"Good riddance?" Marv's fingers closed over the bark. "Four people are dead!"

Seth waved a dismissive hand before reaching for his juice. "Who's next?"

Marv tossed the bark onto his plate, then rubbed his face. "Stop asking me that. How can you even think that I'd—"

"Doing the first one is always the hardest part. You've already done it, so . . . ," Seth reminded him.

Marv sat motionless for a long moment, wanting desperately to disagree, but he wasn't sure what he believed anymore. All he knew was he didn't want to do it again. "I . . . I don't want to kill anyone," he whispered, staring at his food.

"Think of it as eradicating worthless vermin," his friend said. "It couldn't be easier. Just pick a potion, say a few simple words, and—"

"I know . . . voila," finished Marv, flatly. "But is it the right thing to do?"

"An eye for an eye, as the saying goes."

Marv's phone vibrated. He pulled it out to see a photo of the lake from his parents, happy as ever and none the wiser. He pocketed it again. "I guess one more rat couldn't hurt, right?" His shoulder raised. "Like you said, they're just bullies."

Seth straightened. "Wise decision. Let's head for my place and pick a new spell."

Marv placed the dishes in the dishwasher and left a note for his parents.

Back in Seth's room, Marv perused the potion shelves with a more attentive eye. The colors and names intrigued him, which made choosing difficult. Asking Seth for help would teach him nothing. Marv knew he needed to do it alone.

"Remember, you have two bullies left," Seth said as he took down two small cauldrons and a jar of crushed leaves. "I vote we do one for each of them and see what happens."

"I suppose." In the end, Marv chose two vials. *Vanish* and *Peel.* He had no idea what they meant or what harm they would bring but hoped they would make Tracy and Kevin leave him alone without causing undue damage. However, since their friends were dead, the concept held less appeal. His stomach churned. Maybe he should go home, read a good book, and forget any of this had ever happened.

As before, Seth prepared everything, drawing the curtains last. "Ready?"

"I don't know if we should—"

His friend talked over him. "Which potion are you using first?"

Marv held up the *Peel* potion. "This one."

The duo repeated the ceremony. This time, Seth only supervised, ensuring his protégé performed the spell correctly and under his watchful eye. Marv made quick work of the casting, albeit with an altered wish. The stabbing pain returned, ripping through his body like one of Seth's athames, but with less force than before.

Lightheaded, Marv sat on the edge of the bed to regain his strength while Seth set up for the second spell. *Vanish.* Since he hadn't been specific about who each spell was directed at, Marv had no idea who would vanish and who would peel. Or be peeled. He was still uncertain what they even meant. The thought made him shudder.

"Ready," Seth said.

Again, they went. Afterward, Marv felt sick. Doubled over on the edge of the bed, he was surprised when Seth sat next to him and rubbed his back. "Normally, I would never recommend doing two spells back-to-back, but you did a great job. As a reward, I'd like to give you something."

Marv perked up as he moved into a sitting position. Seth handed him a book with a metal cover, one embossed with lines resembling climbing ivy. An old-fashioned latch kept the pages inside secure. A painted green eye stared up from the cover's center.

"This is an ancient spell book I found in a quaint shop in Paris," Seth said, tapping the cover. "There are hundreds of potion recipes in here, including what effects they have, what colors they are, and how they smell. Savor each page. Do not rush through it. Study its wisdom."

Despite his friend's advice and his own worries over the morality of their actions, by the time Marv got home, he'd already flipped through several pages, thirsting for forbidden, ancient knowledge. Images and incantations quickly seared into memory as he absorbed the pages.

By nightfall, he was both exhausted and afraid. What if the new spells worked the way the first one had and another of the Enemy died? Would he be able to live with the knowledge of what he and Seth had done?

Maybe if he did not fall asleep, nothing terrible would happen to Kevin or Tracy. He was happy to stay up all night if he had to, and there was always the book to keep him occupied. Sitting at his desk, he flipped it open, eyes glazing over as page after page turned . . .

Kevin staggered home from a party, the acrid scent of booze seeping from his pores as he stopped for the occasional swig from his whiskey bottle. Drunk, he ranted about his abusive father and sobbed that James was gone. As he weaved along a dark stretch of road, he never saw the misshapen shadow lurking nearby. There were no streetlights. Seconds later, the attack came quickly, oblivious to the boy's drunken mutterings.

Within moments, the ogre carried the broken corpse home, ensuring Kevin's parents would find their precious son in the morning. What better place than their own front yard? Without sympathy, the dark green beast twisted Kevin's body like a balloon animal, pulling his arms and legs from their sockets.

Chuckling a rumble like thunder, the ogre grabbed a garden gnome and shoved it through Kevin's chest, pinning him to a thick oak tree, displaying him like a broken, discarded marionette. Plus, it made the peeling process so much easier. Kevin wouldn't need his skin anymore. Or eyes. Or ears. They were scattered about the lawn, leaving scarlet trails decorating the grass like a horribly gruesome painting. With a final laugh, the beast lumbered away.

Marv lifted his head off the open book and ran toward the bathroom to vomit. As he washed his hands and face, tiny drops of blood escaped from beneath his fingernails and colored the water. He gagged. It wasn't possible.

What he needed, if he could stomach it, was food. He was sure that would make him feel better. With a glance at the clock, he frowned. It was three in the morning. Tiptoeing downstairs, he slunk toward the kitchen, pausing once and again if the floor squeaked.

It dawned on him how odd it was his parents never called him to dinner. His mom would have at least come to his bedroom and found him sleeping—right? Maybe she just did not want to wake him. He opened the fridge and discovered a plate of cold mashed potatoes, gelled gravy, and something resembling roast beef. Marv closed the door with a harsh snap. After that dream, he needed something less stomach-curdling. A handful of cookies would do. Chips would help, as well.

———

That afternoon, his mother insisted on dragging him and his father out for an afternoon bike ride around town, another thing the bullies teased him about. Or used to. After they returned, his dad turned on the football game. Meanwhile, Marv collapsed asleep on the couch and did not see a single play. Thankfully, he had no dreams, but upon waking, his mom mentioned how 'that nice Stuart boy, Kevin' was murdered Saturday night.

His dad shook his head, wearing a disgusted face. "That's too bad." He peered at his son. "Weren't you friends with him?"

Marv never answered. He was already halfway up the stairs, hyperventilating. "It wasn't me. It wasn't me. It wasn't me," he muttered, heading for the bathroom to inspect himself.

Apparently, he thought, the blood under his fingernails was not from his face. It told a different story. But why wasn't there more of it?

———

For dinner, his mom cooked chicken. Marv gagged briefly as his father snapped the thigh bone and drumstick apart to gnaw the bones. Cartilage ripped and was chewed with enthusiasm. Marv thought his dad looked like a caveman finishing a meal after not eating for a week.

Looking away, he focused on the rest of the food, opting for salad, mashed potatoes, and some cheese. Maybe he'd Google how to become vegan. Meat suddenly made him sick.

After a few bites, Marv excused himself, traipsing upstairs to sit on his bed, his back pressed to the headboard. He opened the book on his lap. No way did he want to fall asleep again. This time, he would take notes, focus, and maybe guzzle coffee once his parents went to bed. Once dawn broke, he'd be safe.

He hoped.

Tracy was the one who, in many ways, he hated as much as James or Kevin. She took pleasure in flicking lit cigarettes into Marv's hair, then laughing as he panicked to put it out. Her retribution came under cover of darkness, too. The beast's favorite place to hide itself.

She staggered to her car and stuck her keys in the door as a large, winged gargoyle swooped from the sky to dig his talons into her scalp. Tracy screamed, swatting helplessly at the powerful legs and sharp claws holding her. They soared into the air, climbing high over the trees. As he let her go, her screams echoed in his ears as he watched her fall to splat on the forest floor.

"Dammit!" Marv flung the ancient book to the floor and nearly tripped over it as he stumbled to the bathroom. That was it. No more potions. No more reading. No more Seth. As far as Marv was concerned, Seth could disappear and take the book with him. That boy, creature, or whatever else, was no friend to him.

Monday morning, Marv told his mom he was sick and needed to stay home. It didn't take much convincing. He'd known the dead kids for years, and many would be reeling from the horrific news.

She tucked him into bed and promised to come home and check on him during her lunch break.

Seth texted ten minutes after his parents left. Reluctantly, Marv let him in and was greeted by a rough embrace.

Strangely, the new boy smelled of incense and something familiar. Copper? No, blood, thought Marv.

"Great job, my friend. You've been a busy boy," said Seth, beaming with pride. "Have you been studying that book? The potions helped you try a few new forms," he continued. "Revenge feels good, doesn't it?"

"Revenge? No, Seth, I—"

"You're happy to have two more bullies gone, yes? Voila." He held his hands out at his sides and waved them as though performing a magical act. In effect, he made Marv's sanity take one last curtain call.

Marv headed to the living room to sit on the couch in stunned silence. "It was a dream. Nothing else. Besides, I most certainly can't change into . . . those . . . things. The whole idea is absurd."

In his heart, he was less sure. He recalled the sight of thick, powerful appendages—as though they were his own—ripping the skin from Kevin's body. Screams from the car as James and his friends were impaled by a giant tree branch. Shrieks from Tracy as long talons dug into her skull to drop her from the sky.

"Who's afraid now, loser?" the attacker whispered as it leaned close.

Only it wasn't the attacker. It was Seth grinning like a Halloween jack-o-lantern.

"They were," Marv said softly. His heart thumped. How did he know such things?

The images were incredibly vivid. Had Marv taken on terribly frightening forms to carry out each deed, or had the spell brought forth some otherworldly creature to fulfill his wishes? He returned to reality with a sharp inhale. He studied his hands, wondering if they belonged to an awful beast, a maniacal killer, or an average teenager. Could they all exist in one body?

"What's happening?" whispered Marv, clutching a cushion to his stomach.

"You wanted to make the abuse stop, and you got your wish," Seth said, sitting across from him. "But there is much more to do. There always is."

"How can you say that? This isn't real. I'm no monster."

"Sure you are," he said. "However, stop seeing it as a bad thing. It's a gift to help make the world a better place. Don't you dig it?"

Marv shook his head and pressed the cushion tighter against his abdomen. "Not if I have to become a murderer."

"You murdered six bullies who tormented you. How much more proof do you want? Believe me, it gets easier."

"Did you do the same thing?" Marv asked, his voice faltering. "Change into . . . creatures . . . monsters. Ah, hell, you know what I'm saying."

Seth joined him on the couch, draping an arm around the boy's shoulders. "I told you I did. I'm no liar, but I am old and tired. Soon, it will be my time to leave this world. I've chosen you as my replacement. You're a quick study, if I may add."

Marv shrugged off his embrace and stood, crossing his arms in defiance. "What if I don't want it anymore?"

"Sorry. Remember, in for a penny, in for a pound," Seth said. "Before long, your human emotions dissipate, and killing becomes second nature. All you must do is study your potions, cast your spells, and keep detailed notes. It helps keep your spellcasting straight. Lastly, tell no one. Ever. This is your secret until the time comes to pass everything along to *your* apprentice, just as I've done. I just hope you choose as wisely as I did." He stood. "Come. We have more work to do."

Marv's stomach flipped as the words sunk deeper, yet he followed without a word, which he hoped Seth took for acceptance. But he had a plan of sorts. There was only one way out of the nightmare, and he was tired of being bullied.

Inside, it was just as quiet as always. Marv slowly looked around. Clearly, Seth lived alone. The whole parents thing was just a ruse. Once they reached his room, Marv gazed at the books and potions, searching the labels for the right one. He had to try. Empowerment welled up as he puffed out his chest and kept his voice light.

"I suppose being able to change into other shapes will have advantages," he said, sounding more confident, even proud.

"That's the spirit," Seth said.

Marv picked a potion from the shelf, wondering which would work best. "Okay. If you think I'm the right man for the job, I'll pick up where you left off."

"Bravo!" Seth threw his hands in the air. "Ding, ding! We have a winner."

"I suppose that makes me the new Potion Master." Marv put the vial on the shelf, then saw one several rows further back. He turned it around to see a signal word. *Vanquish.*

"So, who's next," Seth asked for the final time.

Marv only grinned.

PURIFICATION

She was dead. Of that fact, he was sure. Her crimes had been non-existent, save for the multitude of imaginary faults his sick mind could produce. Samuel was not well by any standard, though he performed his daily duties as any other respectable, competent man. Conversely, his mind held torture, cruelty, and despair in high regard, for he had grown accustomed to it.

His childhood had been teemed with misery, abuse, and indecency. Narcotics kept his mother in a vacant, mindless state to the world around her. Most days, she could not recall her own son's name. Father was an awful drunk, which, of course, led to beatings of the worst kind for the slightest infractions. On good days, the man's rants were merely verbal, while others brought black eyes, broken bones, and wounds deeper than anyone would ever discover, even if they hazarded a guess concerning their presence on the boy's body.

In retrospect, Samuel foolishly believed their influence would diminish once distance lay between them. For years, he based several futile escape attempts on such a belief. But to this day, long after their deaths, they still haunted him, constantly forcing him toward a darkened abyss from which none could ever return. Their voices allowed him little rest, coming at all hours, tormenting already fractured sleep, clawing at his mind with constant, hideous untruths of his worth.

Despite prolonged madness, Samuel was not yet so sick as to be without points of clarity. Though he owned none, he maintained a deep love for animals, once having several who reached a natural age before death. Harming living things that gave unconditional love was a line he could never cross. On the other hand, people, with their harsh, hurtful ways, anger, contempt, and treachery, deserved no such reprieve. Both his mother and father served as prime examples.

Samuel was no fool but could not comprehend why others proved themselves to be abhorrent beings regularly. Most days, he believed they secretly mocked him from afar, and he hated them all for their uncaring attitudes and deceptive ways.

Despite his distaste for others, throughout the years, he had taken two lovers, regardless of him being a damaged, hateful man. In his heart, he still held fond memories of each. Both were rare beauties, unsullied by the world's ugliness. Unfortunately, they, too, had vanished from his life. Being of high breeding, one moved away in a hastily arranged marriage after her father suspected Samuel's worsening condition. The other fell unexpectedly ill and died years ago to a cruel malady no doctor could name or cure. The illness ravaged her body until her final, painful day. Samuel never forgot the experience. The event would forever haunt him with fullness of misery and harsh remembrances.

From that day forward, only prostitutes filled his sexual urges. Any desire to expose his heart and true feelings was left firmly in the past. Love was dead to him, just as much as the woman at his feet.

Staring at the body while settled in another moment of lucidity, he understood no fouler deed could have been deliberately fashioned than the act performed minutes prior. But the reckless street walker had made the ghastly mistake of accusing him of withholding her precious money when, in truth, he had left it on the nightstand, unseen as she woke long after their tryst.

As she blamed and berated him, vile offerings from his father overrode her voice to proclaim his son's lack of sexual prowess, stupidity, and failure to do any deed in life correctly. Mother's voice blared in the opposite ear. Her dreadful sound rose shrill and hateful during her diatribe of repulsive insults and demeaning words.

Lost in rage, Samuel seized the woman's throat and tightened his grip, holding unceasingly until she moved no more. Hate, rising from a dark spot he could neither control nor resist, kept him prisoner in its grasp. After taking her corpse sexually once more as an act of insult, he bludgeoned, stabbed, and pummeled the body until the last remnants of strength left him.

Collapsing, he wept as the voices returned. Shouting at them to take their leave proved futile. With both hands pressed to his ears to avoid their harassment, he cast himself on the worn sofa as the world slowly blackened around him. Samuel lapsed into unconsciousness. Though there would be no respite, his parents' words followed, even invading his dreams.

———

The mess, as if the woman's dead, stiffened body was simply a coffee stain on the living room floor, was cleaned away after a bit of breakfast to regain his strength. Her remains, along with the soiled rug she lay stiff on, were dragged to the dank basement where, after considerable dismemberment upon her person, they were tossed into the wood-burning furnace. Her blood sizzled and popped as it boiled away into nothingness. Skin shriveled and disappeared like burning paper. Samuel wondered if the heavy smoke exiting the chimney would draw attention. It was too late to worry about that now.

Scooping out larger bone fragments to place them in a small wooden box, he hauled the pieces to a hidden pit in the backyard where, once buried, they would become forgotten, a thing of the past.

————————

Shortly after the deed was done, a most unexpected turn of events occurred. The door ringer chimed as a visitor—a rarity indeed—spun its handle several times. Samuel rose with no small amount of bewilderment prickling beneath his skin. He quickly gathered his mental faculties, restoring his visage to the reasonable, level-headed man the world was accustomed to seeing.

Mother and Father's voices whispered commands, setting ablaze ideas of murder and mayhem as he took shaky steps to the entry. He peeked through the spy hole only to draw a quick breath.

Not idly did Samuel fall smitten, yet as he peered out, there came the resurfacing of every joy he had ever held. Delight stiffened his body, and another quick breath unmoored him. Several years had passed since a sight rendered him so perplexed, even longer since he was beguiled, and not for the purposes of death.

The unyielding voices, shrouded temporarily by his burgeoning infatuation, came again. Again, Samuel clamped both hands over his ears, wishing to scream aloud and drown out their noise. The ringer chimed once more, its jingling sound proffering a heartfelt emotion that had eluded him since the demise of his last love interest.

After a final straightening, he ran his fingers through his hair, then rechecked his appearance in a nearby mirror. Smiling falsely, he unbolted the heavy locks, swung wide the wooden door, and uttered a greeting.

The lovely woman's perfume wafted in the swirling breeze. Samuel froze, staring open-mouthed as she introduced herself as Mary. A simple enough name, he thought, and one clearly not doing her incredible beauty justice.

Oddly enough, she dressed as a man—a bold statement in these times. No long dress or tight bodice was gracing her well-formed frame. Instead, she displayed tailored pants, an expensive shirt, and a matching, fashionable vest. Completing his surprise was a loose-fitting tie and brown bowler hat.

He remained speechless as he drank in her every inch. Never had he encountered such an anomaly. Could she be as unique as he was, he wondered.

Clicking his heels together, he bowed in gentleman's fashion. "At your service, Miss Mary. How may I help?" He swept an arm to the side. "Please, come in and make yourself at home."

She flowed into the room like a breath of fresh spring air, further captivating him. Samuel followed dumbly, finding it impossible to think or form coherent sentences. Hurriedly recalling proper manners, he offered her a seat on the couch, accompanied by a proposition of refreshment.

Noticing his distress and deeming it rather attractive, Mary blushed as she replied. "I am here on behalf of The Watchers, our neighborhood crime patrol. I assume you know of them?" She waved a hand toward the window with a graceful, practiced movement, then went on before waiting for a reply. "We are exploring last night's disappearance of a young woman—a prostitute from the east side. Could it be you have seen her or know her whereabouts?" Her tone sounded coy, almost seductive. Yet, great strength was contained there, too, he noticed. "Certainly, a man of your obvious stature would wish to help, yes?"

Samuel nearly fainted straightaway. The voices screamed as his wanton gaze roved over her shapely body.

Peering into her eyes was difficult as he felt himself slip into two swirling pools of a fetching green color. Her flowing red hair was like fire from the gods, radiant, as if glowing with energy. He reached for the water pitcher before him, working his mind as best he could.

"A missing woman, you say," he offered calmly while pouring two tall glasses of water. He handed her one with another slight bow as she thanked him. "I recall hearing a visitor knock last evening but did not answer. I was indisposed. By the time I arrived, my stoop was barren."

The corners of Mary's mouth raised, flashing a knowing smile. She leisurely sipped her drink, her eyes never leaving his. "Then may I assume there has been some mistake? Someone, it is unimportant who, made the accusation, believing they saw the missing woman enter your home. Curiously, she never left." She paused long enough to gauge his reaction. "Of course, people regularly err in judgments and observations, though you can plainly see the oddity of the situation. Do you agree?"

Nodding to acknowledge her words, he pondered the dilemma. Anxiety quickly hastened up Samuel's throat like an abhorrent beast clawing its way free. It seemed incomprehensible their arrival had been witnessed, for he went to great lengths to ensure privacy in every detail of his sexual rendezvous. More concerning were questions of whether his actions were being monitored. If such was the case, he could only blame himself. The coincidence was disturbing.

Forceful voices echoed through his skull with talk of his failure. He flinched involuntarily against the unending slights, an action not unnoticed by Mary.

"Was this woman of some importance? Did she carry a status of a sort?" he asked, raising a shoulder unconcernedly.

Mary tilted her head in confusion. "What strange questions to ask," she noted. After studying him further, Mary shook her head. "She was a filthy whore, nothing more. Yet, a human being, nonetheless."

For an instant, Samuel detected her disdain for the subject or for the victim herself. That may work to my advantage, he thought.

The voices rose up. *Kill her. She knows too much, you damnable fool,* yelled his father. *She is playing a game! Kill her now!* cried his mother. Again, he fought them down. He wondered how long he could play this game before tripping over his words and incriminating himself.

"Certainly, your words are true," he noted coolly. "But I must ask if this person somehow bettered our lives? Why spend precious time, likely ill-fated, searching for a woman of the night? Will others mourn her? Possibly several starving children unable to suckle her breasts any longer? A caring husband or family? These things I greatly doubt."

Mary settled deeper into the chair's plump cushions, taken by his bizarre inquiries. "True enough. Your points are valid in their entirety. Still, pressing business brought me to your doorstep, so here we sit." Her eyes took in the neat and orderly room. They lingered by the mantle place longer than the rest. "Personally, I hold a certain, undeniable belief that you have done her grievous harm, likely to death. Evidence supports my theory. And if not the woman in question, certainly you have slain others before her."

Samuel instantly felt sick at her words. Vomit edged up his throat. Refusing to drop his guard, he chuckled, then forced air through his pursed lips in mockery. "Evidence, you say. I further my objection to your accusations since they are repugnant. I also note your rude manners, for you to come to my home, have gained my hospitality, then boldly accuse me of heinous crimes. Of which, I had no part in," he lied as nervousness took control—trembling hands, rapid blinking, and dilated pupils, all of which he hoped went undetected.

Mary moved to the mantle she had eyed, resting an elbow on its surface, still looking at ease. "The blood splatter and brain matter here," she pointed, "and here," another point, this one to the floorboard, "tell a different story." She ran a finger over the higher stain and examined it closely. "These are quite fresh, yes? What say you to that?"

With great effort and welling terror, Samuel realized that while scrubbing the crime area during the pale grey morning light, he had overlooked minuscule aspects of his handiwork. He cursed himself silently for hurrying the task.

The voices missed no chance to show their contempt. His father sounded off at first. *Idiot! Buffoon!* His mother's shrill offerings came next. *Clod! Imbecile!*

Undoubtedly, Mary needed to die now, too, he thought. But what if she had told others of her suspicions before venturing to his home? Sadly, it was an altogether possible scenario. Were those pesky Watchers, who secreted themselves within some dank headquarters to hide their annoying nosiness, discussing his current plight? Would he need to slay them all to keep his secrets safe? He pondered that as he moved closer to his guest. Her death was drawing nigh.

"It seems I have been discovered," he admitted. "Or have I, since I steadily deny my part in this killing you claim I have perpetrated." There was an unmistakable hint of admiration in his voice over her deductions. "Tell me, Miss Mary, where does that leave us?"

She shrugged nonchalantly. "Should you convey any reasonable theory of how your mantle holds bodily matter, I will leave now and never return." She waited, seemingly enjoying their deadly game.

Slowly, his hand moved to the sharp knife hidden lengthwise in the small of his back in a secreted sheath attached to his trouser belt. The strike needed to be quick and clean. This time, he would ensure the results would be thoroughly scrubbed to the last inch. No further mistakes could be made.

Worry over the others who may know of his deeds would come later. The current situation begged to be resolved quickly. Deliberating on taking the life of such a remarkable woman saddened him. Even through his madness, he knew unique qualities when they presented themselves.

The voices rebounded, demanding her unpleasant end as they spouted their usual odious offenses upon his already chaotic mind.

Mere seconds from striking, Mary seemed to sense his game. She moved away, reseating herself on the couch, then indicated the chair with a push of her chin. "You misunderstand my motives, fine sir." Waiting for her host to seat himself, she smiled and went on. "I did not come with intentions of notifying enforcement officers of your deeds. Nor will I inform The Watchers." She leaned forward, her face demure, yet her eyes bore an unmistakable intensity. "No, indeed. Factually, I have come to join you."

Tempered delight simmered within Samuel's soul, though he remained uncertain if her words bore the tiniest fragments of truth or were complete embellishments. Perhaps the voices played a cruel trick? Mayhap the crafty vixen laid a skillfully deceptive trap. Did she work for The Watchers, or had she aligned herself with the police? Both? Maybe neither. He shifted to cross his legs, portraying more fictitious ease with his situation, though his stomach was knotted. Again, bile rose in his throat.

"First, you spin a most spectacular tale of homicide. Now, you claim to hold a desire to join me. If any of your words are true, why would trust be placed firmly in your lap at the drop of a hat? I have known you no longer than the life span of a fruit fly."

"You have already admitted your crime in as much as the words you have uttered," she replied. "Further, you give no explanation of the mantle."

Silently, he cursed several times, having already forgotten that part. The voices chastised him once more, though he nervously laughed them away. "I have done no such thing. Pray tell you know a jest when you hear one?" To derail the probing questions, he turned to interrogating her. "Why would one so lovely and intelligent wish to participate in such monstrously foul acts?"

Mary sipped her water, then, in proper fashion, dabbed her full lips with a napkin. "You are fully aware that humans are a disease in many ways. And like any such illness, must be cured by whatever means necessary."

Such a veiled response warranted caution, but only after Samuel entertained the prospect of continuing with a partner by his side. His wishes, now recognized as a profound longing to carry out his murderous plans, balanced on a precipice, making him dizzy.

"Forgive my boldness, but you have not answered my previous

inquiry," he said, able to speak again. "You do not seem a murderess. Explain your motivations. Why willingly perform odious deeds?"

At some length, Mary's story spilled out, paralleling with remarkable similarity Samuel's own twisted life. Her sprawling account returned him to darkened places where repressed memories tortured his soul and his parents' haunting voices. He flinched at the agonizing scenes as they played in his head. He found himself clenching his teeth.

She generally expressed disdain over humans to his bliss, with few exceptions. Like her host, former experiences soured her outlook.

Before this day, aspirations of finding another who understood him had long since vanished, sunken deep within the gloom of misery. Yet, a suitable companion was present and mere feet away, rekindling a flame of hope in finding a kindred spirit.

Her story reached its end with a simple inquiry. "Shall we join forces?" she asked.

Samuel had been purifying humans for some time, but his vision could become vividly honest with a partner. Mary had cemented his belief that he had been right in thinking humans were a disease.

He ran both hands over his face and sighed. Madness subsided enough to envision a future of ridding the streets of the foul, wretched things walking near him. Addicts, drunkards, abusers, haters, and more needed cleansed.

His brow raised at the final word. Cleansed. That was his hope. Maybe then, mother and father would take a semblance of pride in their only son, especially since they shared no such sentiment while alive. Would a murderous spree quiet them once and for all?

"Fancy I accept your terms, what would come of it? An equal partnership in this adventure you say I currently pursue. Furthermore, would you expect remuneration for such deeds, of which there would be little from my tightly held funds?"

Mary waved away his concern with another graceful turn of her hand. "To that point, I hold a great deal in reserve and have substantial assets—a benefit of wealthy parents, I daresay. They have since moved to their next lives, leaving me alone. I will share all with you for inclusion into your Purification." She paused, considering her words. "I rather like that name. It holds a special feel. Don't you agree?"

Samuel nodded stupidly. In truth, the question had not mattered, for he would have agreed to anything she hinted at or suggested. He was beside himself with envy and burgeoning love. Mary was the most astonishing woman he had ever met. Gorgeous in appearance, wealthy in finances, fit in body, suitable for sexual activity, and most notable, a palpable desire to rid unfit humans from the planet.

As the voices began once more, he forced them away for the last time, giving angry, unspoken instructions never to darken his mental doorway again. Never again did he wish to hear their insufferable criticisms ringing in his ears. He had found his life's calling, and they would not be included in his joy. Time for Purification was at hand.

BROKEN BONDS

A ttics smell awful and are rather dusty. They are inherently replete with stale air and lingering heat. Conversely, basements are cold, dank, creepy places—barely more acceptable than the former. But those facts mattered little since Michelle and Edgar would be cleaning both.

Their chores were punishment for sneaking out during the night. However, neither brother nor sister perceived any misconduct in their daring feats. After all, they derived great pleasure in routinely visiting the local cemetery— joking the dead were far more interesting than those living. They relished adventure.

Both parents were displeased despite their children's reasonings or feeble attempts to object. Their recourse was to banish their children to grandma's house for the summer. Naturally, the plan backfired since the siblings adored their mother's mother. She was sweet, treated them like adults, and offered the respect they sought. A social feature the duo rarely received at home.

If forced to spend a few summer vacation days cleaning as punishment, so be it. The teens agreed they could easily handle that part. Besides, the objects they discovered in the attic and basement were well worth their efforts. There were dusty boxes of old swords, lovely clothing from long ago—Gothic or Victorian era were their guesses—and steamer trunks laden with stickers from around the world. Opulent jewelry boxes, posh baubles, curious photos, and more piqued their interest. However, the most precious piece was a small, ornate, locked box that fascinated Edgar. Desire to view the contents burned in his heart, though he never mentioned it to Michelle.

After the day's chores, Edgar snuck back to the attic, took up the box, picked the lock, and opened the lid with great anticipation. Sadly, wonder turned to disappointment at discovering nothing more than a few old coins. Despite this, on further inspection, he understood the coins were unique. Each was placed correctly in its own circular depression atop a dark, purple velvet cloth lining the inside. He plucked one out.

The size of a modern silver dollar, it fit neatly in his palm. There were twelve in all. Oddly, as he handled them in turn, each grew warm to his touch, though never became overly hot or uncomfortable. The strangest detail was the embossed faces. None were of any king, queen, or president he had ever seen. These are not for spending, he thought.

Instead, the images were monster-like, with horned heads, fangs, or twisted faces. Some even appeared as vicious beasts, like those Edgar had often read about in Grimm's Fairytales or other scary books.

Mesmerized by the newly discovered treasures, he tucked the box away, secreted it to his room, then spent hours exploring the mysterious objects. Like the scary raised impressions, the composition was unlike any he had ever seen. They were not cast from gold, silver, brass, or iron. The strange material was entirely foreign.

Time passed as he puzzled over them long into the night. After a long while, sleep took him deep into fitful dreams.

Bleary-eyed, he sat at the breakfast table, wondering if he looked as awful as he felt.

His sister was unabashedly staring. "You look like shit. Did you sleep at all?"

Great! I do look as horrible as I feel, he thought.

"Language, please," came Grandma's voice from behind. She was cooking breakfast. Minutes later, she shuffled to the table to slide eggs onto their plates, followed by golden hashbrowns and small, fluffy pancakes. "There's plenty of syrup and butter on the table. Eat well. I'm off to the store for groceries and to visit a friend. I may not be back for a while."

Michelle perked up. "It is a man-friend, Grandma?" she chided. "It's been years since grandpa died. You need a good stiff—"

"Drink," interrupted Edgar, scowling at his sister, knowing exactly what her mind was on—sex. It was all she had on her mind lately, he mused. "She was saying you need a stiff drink to help you relax a bit."

Grandma blushed as she folded her apron, draping it over the chair back. "Never you mind my business, Mister and Miss Nosy. Don't destroy my house or wander off, please. I love you both. Behave."

With that, she kissed their cheeks, grabbed her purse, and then closed the front door as she left.

"What are you thinking!" cried Edgar, throwing his hands in the air. "You weren't going to suggest grandma get laid, were you?" He huffed.

"Relax, Turbo! I was going to say . . . okay, you got me. But she does need to get laid," said Michelle. "She would sleep better."

Edgar laughed, shoved pancake pieces in his mouth, and chewed quickly. "You totally suck. No wonder we're always in trouble." He laughed again, dug in his pocket, then tossed a coin on the table. "What do you make of that?"

Michelle drew in a quick breath and slowly let it out. "Hold on! Where did you get this?" Her brows furrowed as she studied the dark coin. "You've been sneaking around in the attic, haven't you? Soon, a smile turned up the corners of her mouth. "It's awesome! I want it!"

"Hold on, sticky fingers. That one is mine! I do have the whole set, though." He scratched his head. "At least, I think I do."

Her eyes widened. "Why is it getting warm?" Her tone turned to amazement. "What else does it do? Are they part of a board game? Or is this another one of your stupid tricks?"

Edgar shrugged, swallowed his eggs, and then held out his hand. Michelle frowned but returned the trinket all the same. He placed the coin back into his pocket and patted it. "No trick. I swear. And I have no idea what it does, where it comes from, or what the faces mean. I just know they are really cool. Let's clean up, and I'll show you the rest."

Minutes later, the pair sat on Edgar's bed with their new possessions spread before them. Examining each in turn, they remained confused, no closer to understanding the origin or purpose of their find.

"We could always ask grandma. They are *hers*, you know," suggested Michelle.

"Right," said Edgar with a sarcastic tone. He stood to pace, waving his arms around to dramatize his point. "By the way, Grandma, I found this cool wooden box in your attic. I took it, picked the lock, lifted the coins, and, oh, yeah, wondered if it's okay for me to keep them. Can you tell me more about them?"

Michelle slapped her forehead. "Shit! You didn't tell me you stole the whole thing."

Edgar nodded as a frown spread over his face. "I know. Sorry about that." He lowered onto the bed again. "Let's forget how I got them." Their eyes met. "Should I put them back?"

Her answer was immediate. "Are you nuts? Of course not. They are probably the coolest thing I've ever seen." She rubbed her palms together as a mischievous light lit her face. "I want to know what they do."

"Me, too." He lifted the box lid and took a small parchment from its depths. "This was there, too, but I can't read it."

Michelle studied the words, trying to sound them out. "Monitum! Periculum! Numquam aperire ne malum effugium." She frowned. "Is that Greek? Roman? Latin, maybe?"

"You're the scholar. You should know what it says." He winked at her playfully.

Seating herself at the small desk, Michelle tapped the keyboard to wake the computer, then began online research. Within minutes, she waved Edgar to her side. They stared at the screen together. "The words are Latin. It reads: Warning! Danger! Never open lest evil take you." She faced him. "Great. Of all the things you could find, you grab evil coins. And you were stupid enough to open it. Why do you always do that?"

He forced air from between his lips. "That's idiotic. Coins can't be evil. That's just plain stupid." Edgar handed a different coin to his sister. "That one can be yours," he said with a sly grin. "It sort of looks like you, too."

She punched his arm. "We can't have the same parents. There's no way we are related. You are a complete dork." She placed it in her pocket and returned to the screen.

———

They debated for some time, with Edgar arguing the coins had most certainly never done harm. Could they be like Aladdin's lamp fable? Did they need to rub them profusely to get wishes granted or make a genie appear? No, that sounded rather childish. Strangely, as time passed, unexplained worry took root in his heart.

"What do these things do?" he asked, more to himself than his sister.

"Maybe we need to say some old magical spell or phrase to make them work," suggested Michelle, wriggling her fingers as if performing an invocation. "Still, that warning freaks me out a little."

He nodded in agreement. "Not that I believe in that stuff, but you could be right. It's too bad we haven't found any words or markings to help us. And I'm more interested in what happens if we make them work."

"Good point." Michelle sat silent for a minute. "You know, it could be a puzzle box. They've been around a long time." She took up the container and carefully felt each inch of the rectangle, her fingers nimbly probing the wooden exterior. Nearly giving up hope, a soft click drew her attention as a hidden drawer popped open.

They gasped in unison as Michelle extracted yet another parchment. She attempted to read it but struggled terribly with the ancient tongue. "A negotio perambulante in tenebris. Ego et socii naves aedificavimus. ¡Siempre y eternamente! Tantum mors vinculum nostrum subvertet."

She rolled her eyes in frustration. "Like I know what all that means, or even how to say any of it." They returned to the computer for more research.

Results came in moments. Edgar read the translation on the screen. "Come from darkness into light. I accept you now. My body is yours forevermore. Our bond shall never be sundered except in death." He flipped the coin in the air to catch it as he began to pace again. "Look up the coins themselves."

Taking several minutes, Michelle leaned closer to the screen. "Wow! Leave it to you to find some cursed shit. Look!" She moved to allow Edgar to have the chair.

He sat for a time, reading, going from site to site. 'Every site says they're ancient, evil, and cursed." He sprang from his chair, arms extended, his face twisted. "Boo!" he shouted.

Michelle jumped, then punched his arm for a second time. "You're a total ass!"

He stepped back. "Sorry, I couldn't resist. I'll admit this is some weird shit. But it's all fake. I'm telling you, a coin cannot be evil."

"Let's quit for tonight," she offered.

Edgar ignored her. Taking his seat, he pushed the speaker icon and listened to the AI repeat the Latin words as he parroted them. After a great many attempts, he was pronouncing the Latin phrase perfectly. Retrieving the coin from his pocket, he held it loosely.

Michelle placed a hand over his. "Listen, I don't think this is a good idea. Let's forget the whole thing and put them back. Grandma will never know," she said, restating her earlier idea.

Edgar pulled back, ignoring her concerns. "If I turn into a demon or the devil, you may want to run."

"Knock it off. This isn't funny anymore. We don't know what we're messing with. Those warnings are probably there for a reason, Einstein."

He scowled and waved a dismissive hand. "Weren't you always the adventurous one? All this mumbo jumbo is just weird superstition from back in the day. Those people were scared of everything they couldn't explain. This is totally harmless, I'm sure." Holding the coin with the horned demon on its surface, Edgar recited the words.

––––––––––

Edgar never felt the swift change as his consciousness fled for some long time before a feeble sense of existence took hold. Thoughts sluggishly formed as his eyes fluttered open, absorbing the dull grey of reality. Prickling sensations moved from head to toe. Some waves felt pleasurable, while others brought a painful grimace and made him cry out.

Blood pounded in his head. His temples thumped as if repeatedly striking a bass drum. Struggling to focus, his eyelids quivered as they attempted to pry themselves open. Finally, as mental wonderings and wretchedness fled, he realized all was dark, save for a singular torch placed in an iron wall scone mere feet before his body.

Where was Michelle? Grandma? The house? He pondered how he had come to be lying on his back. He had been standing erect before. Nothing made sense. How long had it truly been since he and his sister had been together? Was this all a twisted dream?

Turning his head as his sight adjusted to the gloom, he guessed he now resided in a gothic manner. The architecture bore out his idea. Rose-shaped, stained-glass windows abounded. Yet he thought there was no light outside to display the magnificence they unquestionably held. The ceiling rose high above, reaching an apex in the form of towering pinnacles. He could not see most since a great deal vanished in the darkness. The chamber held scattered but neatly organized furnishings. Those, he could hazily see.

Believing he was not alone, he strained his hearing. Suddenly, braziers of fire sprang to life, spurring the young man to action. Raising to a crouched position, he stared at the flickering orange flames, imagining who had lit them. There was no one. He was isolated, confused, and scared.

"Who's there?" he shouted in a voice sounding much unlike his own. It shocked him, though there was no time to consider the anomaly. He endeavored to regain full use of his wits.

Silence fell again, save for the crackling sounds of the dancing flames. Radical impulses took hold as Edgar wished to flee. To his dismay, he held no viable idea of which direction to travel should he follow his instinct to preserve his health.

Then, his world imploded in many ways. As he stepped toward the braziers, placed throughout the room on heavy iron tripod stands, it dawned that his footsteps sounded quite heavy. Clumsy, he thought.

Passing a dark mirror that hung beside a wide, stone, arched entrance, he recoiled at the sight as he peered into the blackened glass. Staring back, displaying as much shock as he felt, was a demon's face. Its large, grey body—like one of a gigantic stone gargoyle—was muscular and fierce looking.

He reeled, alight with fear, halting once the image vanished from sight. Calling up all the bravery he could muster, he edged forward again. The demon returned, as well.

"Who are you!?" shouted Edgar. "What do you want of me?"

In that horrible moment, the young man also realized words came from the demon's mouth. The beast repeated his utterances and mimicked his actions. How? he wondered. Moving a hand to pinch himself, ensuring this was no dream, he saw a giant, clawed appendage rising from his side.

Again, he reeled, trying desperately to escape the dreadful arm, to be clear of its long reach. He rounded hard, expecting to see his tormentor facing him. But the room lay empty. Slowly, he closed his eyes and raised an arm to shoulder level. Preparing himself, he flung both eyelids open, only to scream at the sight.

The grey, long arm belonged to him. Rushing to the mirror, he tore it from its mount, set it on the floor to lean against the stone wall, then backed away to take in the full view.

Shock and terror brought tears to his eyes as he stared at a beast he knew all too well. He had seen it before—at least the head was known. The image was identical to the embossed coin he once carried in his pocket.

Now, long limbs hung by his sides, grey skin was pulled taut over a heavily muscled body, and enormous feet were attached to thick, powerful legs. Two blackened horns protruded from his head. He felt them in disbelief.

"What's happening!" he screamed, running forward to kick the mirror. Shattered fragments filled the air, tinkling with resonating sounds as they landed. "This isn't real!"

"I assure you, it is quite real," came a soft, calm voice.

Edgar spun to see his former self. A handsome young lad stared back. It was his exact likeness, down to the long scar on the back of his hand from a misadventure with a knife during his youthful days. Thick black hair was parted perfectly, and both eyes looked as lively and bright as his were before this nightmare.

"I have waited centuries to be released," said the youth, running his hands over his body, feeling it for the first time. He gave a royal, sweeping bow. "I owe you my life."

"How did you do this? Are you a god?" cried Edgar. "Give my body back. It isn't yours."

The false Edgar chuckled. "But it is," he said coolly. "You read the words willing, thus allowing us to make the transference. Now, you shall remain here in what will become your home until the end of time. Unless, of course, some other fool discovers the coin and reads the spell. Then, you can be free as I am now."

Michelle entered his mind for an instant. *Please don't let her read those words. By the gods, keep her safe.* He snapped back to the present. "I didn't transfer shit! Get out of my body, you freak!" Edgar charged, his clawed limb raised to strike, but his inhuman counterpart raised a hand, bringing him to a halt.

"Lash out if you must. But here in this place, we are unable to harm one another. We can not die by another's hand or do malice upon ourselves."

Willpower flowed from Edgar. He slumped against the wall and lowered to rest on his haunches. His large head leaned on his thick limbs. "This can't be real. I'll wake up any second. Michelle will save me." He instantly regretted the thought of relying on his sister for help. Then, she would be in danger, too.

As if summoned, the young woman appeared. She looked quite like herself, and, thankfully, carried the broadsword from the attic. It seemed too large for her, but she wielded it nonetheless. Her eyes moved betwixt the demon and the false, tricksy version of her brother. Confounded by her situation, instinctively going from appearances alone, she gave a war cry. She charged the demon as he extended his arms.

"Stay back, Edgar!" she cried. "I'll save you."

"No, Michelle, no!" cried the real Edgar, his knobby limbs held outward to stop her advance. "I'm your brother!"

Regrettably, the sound she heard was harsh to her ears, coming in a language she could not possibly comprehend. Demon speech. It flowed from his thick lips, rough, as one would imagine a demon's voice to be.

Without thinking, he rushed to embrace her, to make her understand the dilemma.

All the while, the actual demon in Edgar's form urged her. "That thing tried to kill me," the lad screamed, pointing at the monster. "Kill it! It's evil."

"No, no, no," retorted her brother, waving his thick, muscled arms again. "Please, help. Sis, I am trapped in here." He pounded his chest, appearing aggressive. Hurriedly, his sentence fell away as his sister charged. Backing away to avoid conflict, he struck the wall and could go no further.

Sadly, the sharp, shining steel passed through his heart in that awful moment. Gasping for air, he staggered to the side, dropped to his knees, then collapsed in a heap.

"No! Please," he uttered a final time as the harsh sounds burst from his throat.

In an instant, Michelle was on him, hacking and hewing until he was entirely dead. The final blow sent his head rolling across the dark marble tile, coming to rest at Edgar's feet. The deceitful demon stared at it, hiding his smile before raising his eyes to meet the young lady. Wiping his eyes in a false display of relief and affection, he ran to throw both arms around her, hugging her closely.

"You're my hero," he said. "That thing nearly destroyed me." He pushed his chin to Edgar's mutilated form. "Well done!"

"What happened? How did I even get here?" She pointed to the ground.

Again, Edgar indicated the headless form. "He summoned you in hopes of killing us both. That way he could enter our world and none would be the wiser. That is what the coins are for: to open the gateway and make the transference. Once the spell was spoken, the magic was released."

Michelle's mind reeled as it rushed past the word 'transference.' Little could she comprehend its meaning presently. Perhaps with more time and different circumstances, she may have understood. But it was not this day. "I never touched one of the coins once you said the spell. You disappeared right after you said the words."

"Too true," replied the false Edgar. "Shall we remedy that? I know how to fix this mess. But you must trust me. Do you still have the coin I gave you? Is it with you now?" There was a hint of excitement in his voice.

Michelle nodded. "Yes, the same one you gave me. But I never did anything with it."

Edgar extended a hand. "May I see it, please. It serves a vital function now."

She produced the coin from her pocket to slip it into his awaiting palm. "But I don't—"

"Perfect!" he interrupted. Earlier, once the false demon switched bodies with the real Edgar, the youth's memories transferred to the monster in the wicked process. With a look of elation, he stroked the image with loving care as he held the coin tightly. "Do you still have the paper? The spell? Give it to me."

She nodded, then scowled at his tone. "I think so." Digging in her pocket again, she held it before her.

"Read it, please. I'm still a bit wobbly from all this stimulation. Plus, I need to ponder the words as you speak them. I think they will help us escape this place."

After a grimace, she agreed. "I'll do it, but I'm not happy about the idea. In fact, I hate it. Our situation has been no good since we found that stupid piece of paper. Not to mention that box." She cleared her throat, hesitated as her eyes went to the head at her feet, then read. "Come from darkness into light. I accept you now. My body is yours forevermore. Our bond shall never be sundered except in death."

As the torches flared, as if lamp oil had been poured on their flames, a new demon stood in the room. This new creature seemed as baffled and petrified as Michelle's brother had been minutes earlier. Her twisted form stood feet from the false Edgar. As her brother had done during his ordeal, she stared into the eyes of another human version of herself.

Michelle screamed as she inspected her new demon form. The transference was complete. She was trapped in a beast's body as her former self grinned wickedly at her.

"The time to rise has come again, my love," said the new Michelle, running her hands over Edgar's chest.

"No!" cried Michelle from across the room. "It can't be." Her eyes went to the hewed pile of flesh she left in her wrathful wake. "Edgar," she whispered. "I didn't know. I am so sorry." Tears trailed down her cheeks as she knelt beside her dismembered brother.

With her back turned, she never saw the blade that severed her head from her shoulders. Her cranium flew in the air like her brother's had done, to land with a grotesque slap. The head rolled next to Edgar's to stare outward like a twisted, matched pair.

The evil Michelle and Edgar kissed. "Their pitiful world is ours now. Shall we go claim it for our own?" asked Michelle.

"Indeed, now that all bonds have been broken," answered Edgar. "First, let us rouse the others. Since we have corporeal bodies, there is no longer a need for those ridiculous coins. They are useless. We shall free them all." A broad smile stretched his mouth wide. "The human race will pay for imprisoning us."

DARKNESS

Darkness holds terror. Since the dawn of man, we have grown to fear shadows and places our vision cannot venture. For hidden there are dreadful specters, countless monsters, and unnamed things lurking in wait to reveal themselves during the wee hours of the night. They come to haunt, frighten, bite, and gnaw. In certain instances, they bring far worse.

Many remain horrifyingly eclipsed from view, appearing only during a quick turn of the head or from the corner of one's eye. Most are unrecognizable, yet some are in their disturbing guises—stunted, twisted beings of all shapes and proportions—things that do not belong to our world as we know it. These creatures conjure up dread, the sight of them thrusting the observer beyond all reasonable semblances of sanity.

Likewise, unfamiliar sounds can instill or add to our endless anxiousness of the obscure. Are tales of monsters, beasts, and creatures nothing more than vivid imaginings stemming from primal fear? We can only dare to guess.

Since early childhood, Rand held a certain foreboding over the darkness. To him, abnormal noises and visions were common, often disallowing any aspect of sleep. Recently, the number of nightmarish instances increased. Gleaming, hateful eyes began to emerge through his opaque world of shadows. Red or yellow, they appeared in different locations within his room or house but consistently remained present. Within days of his latest sightings, one pair became two, then three, four, and more. It was akin to being a caged animal within a zoo exhibit. His privacy, and perhaps sanity, were being violated.

Though these creatures never drew close enough to touch, their whispering voices filled his bed chamber with unintelligible, horrid sounds. Some clambered over his bed. He knew from the shifting of his covers and bounce of the mattress.

Typically, he lay motionless, clutching the intricate golden amulet his grandparents had given him as if it offered protection as he hid beneath the sheets. Too panicked to peek out from his security, he shivered with uncontrollable fright. Then, after a long while, he heard the things leap onto the floor and shuffle away. Afterward, the closet door would mysteriously latch close. He hated the closet and never drew near its door after dusk. Even in daylight hours, dread filled him if required to venture inside its depths.

During these nocturnal encounters he became proficient at studying sounds to guess the creatures' activities. Often, they revealed their locations by chairs squeaking or books falling from shelves. Only when silence grew to a hush would his eyes snap open to find nothing more than a faint moonglow lighting his room.

Rand attempted to share his concerns, only to be rebuffed. His parents gave him nothing more than assurances he had been dreaming or employing his potent imagination. Schoolmates scoffed at his words. No one would listen. However, Clarissa, Aurora, and Evan were the exceptions, for their experiences closely mirrored his own. Were they special? Or were they cursed? He was inclined to believe the latter.

Evan vanished two weeks prior. He had been seen by a neighbor stepping into the forest late in the evening. That same night, the boy's father had taken up a lantern and searched for his son, and he, too, vanished without a trace. Finally, after five sequential days of searching, the patrolling volunteers and constables discovered both sets of barely recognizable remains scattered about the entrance to the old local castle.

Naturally, rumors flew over the cause of their demise, but Rand knew what had happened. Or so he suspected. The beastly night creatures had killed them. They likely had Clarissa, too, since her disappearance came less than twenty-four hours ago and was eerily similar. Despite his fear, Rand vowed to find her before she met the same fate as Evan and his father.

Aurora lived on the outskirts of the village. Once Rand approached, she hefted her pack onto her shoulder and fell in step with his assured footfalls. Together, they headed toward the woods.

Her pack consisted of light food, matches, and torches, while Rand's old rucksack held an extra coat and large hunting knife pilfered from his father's closet. Being prepared was a source of pride for him, and he saw no harm in the minor act of thievery. Besides, he would return it, he thought. Providing, of course, he lived through the night.

By early morning, as time approached the nine o'clock hour, the duo neared the castle, the usual meeting place of the foursome. They stood within yards of the entrance where the remains had been discovered.

The structure seemed different as it peered down with an unspoken gloom, as though the castle walls were engrossed with the horror enacted here. Yet beauty abounded, as well. Large stained-glass windows were nestled within enviable stone and mortar work. Arched cathedral roofs crowned with pointed spires, stout stone buttresses, and stylishly woven corbels graced the exterior.

Nevertheless, unexplained dizziness gripped Rand as vague horror took his thoughts. After all, another friend may be discovered dead, perhaps mere feet from where they stood. With two already murdered, the chances Clarissa was alive were next to none. Yet they could not falter now.

Aurora shivered. "This place used to be so special to me. But now it feels creepy since . . ." Her words faded as she fashioned her long brown hair into a ponytail as if avoiding the thought. Her face contorted from disgust. "Look." She pushed her chin forward, directing Rand's eyes to the entrance.

Though the dead bodies had been removed, a surplus of blood-stains remained. Crimson splatter speckled the opening and landing. Innards, or possibly brain matter, still adhered to the doorframe. All pointed to a savage attack. Rand stepped before her to display a thin smile and touch her forearm.

"Stay here, please. I'll take a look. There's no need for you to see this," he said quietly, jerking a thumb over his shoulder.

She shook her head. "Seeing where they died will not help either of us. And I have a thought. We can use the servants' entrance and get in that way." Her eyes silently pleaded with him.

"Wonderful idea," he conceded with a nod, taking her hand before moving toward the southern wing with its curved, heavy wooden door.

Several weeks ago, as the group awaited the perfect time to sneak inside, they noticed the groundskeeper going about his duties. At day's end, he hid a spare key beneath a grotesque's tongue—a place most would not dare search. This day, the duo quietly entered using the hidden key to slip inside. They slid the thick bolt into place and locked the door behind them. Rand pocketed the key.

Even on this cloudless sunny day, the hall remained hazy, for only dim light reached within the recesses of the thick walls. The darkened walls extended in either direction. The shadows, appearing first as undulating waves of pitch black, stretched spindly, clawed extremities to pierce and torment their skin.

Rand's eyes bounced left and right as he tried to remain in the middle of the carpeted floor. Pressing gloom covered the edges of their vision, which sprung a panicked fear that slowed their advance, enticing his imagination to conjure evil beasts at every turn.

Aurora shuddered from the chilled air. "I wish Evan and Clarissa were here."

"Me, too." Rand placed an arm around her shoulder and hugged her close. "You're safe with me." The words sounded confident and robust, as intended, but his innards flipped. His body lacked the same conviction as fear welled in his heart.

"Do you really believe Clarissa would have come here?" asked Aurora softly. "What exactly do you want to find?"

Not wishing to dash her hopes, he ignored the first question. Instincts told him Clarissa may not be found at all, let alone alive. Still, he told himself he had to keep hope and remain optimistic. "Two people already died here, and I think the constables did a horrid job investigating. This may be our only chance to find a clue concerning their deaths," replied Rand. "And Clarissa always felt safe in this place. So, yes, I think she could be here." He stopped to hang his head and sigh. "The day she vanished, she had asked me to come along, but I had to go to a local play with my folks. I'm to blame. I should have been with . . ."

Aurora touched his cheek and frowned. "Then you would be missing, too, and I would be alone. This is not your fault."

"Tell that to my heart," added Rand, glancing at an enormous painted portrait of a stately, well-dressed gentleman whose eyes seemed to follow their every move. A chilled sensation swept past as they stood, spurring him to proceed quicker.

Breathlessly, they entered a long hall, then the kitchen. It was frigid.

Wind leaked through small cracks and crevices to jangle the hanging pots and pans suspended over the tall butcher block.

Aurora shrieked quickly, then placed a hand over her mouth as if trying to hold the sound back. She raised a shoulder and looked sheepish. "Sorry about that. I'm a bit nervous."

"Quite fine," he replied. "It rattled me, too."

She chuckled for a moment before her face lost all color. Extending an arm, she pointed ahead to a lengthy hallway.

Rand gave a quick inhale. A clump of blue lay several feet from them, flecked with the green yarn Clarissa had knitted in herself. It was her favorite scarf. Rand hurried forward, dropping to his knees as a tear dribbled down his cheek. Picking up the soft material, he clutched it to his chest and rose.

So intent was he on their friend's scarf that the boy failed to notice what it lay near—an end table on which stood a frightening sight. A loathsome creature with pointed teeth, sharp claws, and long, thick limbs glowered over him on the pedestal. Open-mouthed, with snarling lips, its orange body stood crouched.

With a practiced flip of his coat hem, he shoved a hand behind his back to free his knife from its sheath. But even with the blade at its throat, the beast never moved.

"This was not here the last time," Rand said, lowering his weapon to examine the creature. "Who would have done something like this? The caretaker?"

She shrugged. "Who knows or cares. It is awfully gross." Summoning her mettle, she took several steps forward to study the creature curiously. "What *is* it?" she questioned. "It looks like one of the things from my—"

"Bedroom," he interjected. "I've seen a similar one, too. At least, I think so." With a trembling hand, he poked the creature's body. Its leathery, rough form remained motionless. He tried again before stowing the knife. "I wonder how we see them, and others do not."

"Maybe we're not supposed to see them," suggested Aurora. "Think about it. Only people who believe they exist or admit to seeing them are disappearing."

Rand pondered her words. "But does that mean Evan's dad saw them? Or did he simply get in their way while snooping around outside?" He scratched his head, considering the awful thought for a moment. "I can't believe he saw the creatures all this time and never said a word?" A sudden edge of anger bordered his next words. "If so, Evan's death would be partly his fault. If he knew his son saw these abominations, why didn't he mention it?"

Aurora shrugged in reply as she searched their surroundings with an apprehensive expression. "I wonder how many people *do* see these creatures and stay silent. They're probably afraid of being labeled insane or having their reputations ruined. I have to be honest. I'm scared witless and do not wish to wind up like Evan—a bloodstain by the entrance."

Rand swallowed hard. "Me neither." He placed the scarf in his rucksack and waved Aurora forward. "I do wonder why we haven't found more signs of Clarissa. She was here."

"Was the scarf planted to throw us off, or do you think she's dead?"

He frowned. "I hate thinking so, but I see no evidence to suggest otherwise. Who would plant the scarf? It makes no sense." Glancing into the darkened corners, he rubbed his hands together in nervous anticipation. "I will admit it feels better knowing others see these nightmares, too. I thought I was going mad. These monsters sow death to all who know of them." His visage turned apologetic. "I am very sorry you are included in that bunch."

"At least I am not alone. I have you to lean on. Nevertheless," Aurora added with a note of defiance, "I want to send these atrocities back to whatever vile place they came from."

They stepped forward with caution, inching toward a heightened degree of silence. The castle was eerily quiet save for their boots tapping softly against the cold marble. Rand wished to call for Clarissa to hear *something* in this hushed void, but to do so would mean instant danger. He would not announce his presence like a fool in case the beasts were here.

Several steps later, a sliver of something bright caught his eye. Relieved, Rand turned toward it, then froze. Ahead, on blurred edges of dull sunlight peering through a great window, he saw a slightly ajar portion of the wall. It lay at the hall's end.

He sucked in a quick breath. "A secret passage!" he whispered.

Aurora's eyes followed his. "I see it, too." She wavered. "But it doesn't lead to any place good. I can feel it."

Taking great care, he wedged his fingers into the opening and pulled, gagging as a foul odor arose from its depths. The acidic aroma reminded him of burnt vinegar. Aurora heaved a retch from behind. Grimacing, he opened the panel wider.

Inside lay a gulf of utter blackness no light dared penetrate. Its silence and stillness sent Rand's soul into a spiraling descent of nameless horror. He imagined the vile creatures swarming over him, their odious scents filling his pores. The taste of their gruesomeness coated his throat and stung his eyes.

Aurora turned away before stepping into the murky opening, busying herself by lighting the torches. As the flames sprang to life, she handed him the brightest one.

"This should help," she said, letting her hand slide over his.

He nodded a silent thanks.

They crossed the threshold and began the terrible, winding descent into places dark, unknown, and best left alone. But that was not their intention this day. Rescuing Clarissa was the goal, one which seemed frustratingly out of reach.

Within a few steps, Rand slipped, struggling to keep balanced, grasping at whatever hold he could gain. In an instant, Aurora was there to steady him.

He waved the torch toward his feet only to discover several blood-stained stairs. There lay small bits of the caretaker. Like Evan, the poor man had been torn to shreds with only pieces of bodily material and his familiar set of keys left behind. The pair retched again as they hurriedly scooted by, pressing their backs hard to the wall as they passed.

The downward gradient seemed limitless. Rand became nauseated with each touch of the damp stones. Straining his eyes through the gloom brought no answers. As with the entrance, the torchlight fought an endless battle to push back the inky blackness.

Deeper they went until time and reality vanished from comprehension. Finally, as the ground leveled, they rounded a corner into a smooth, black-stoned chamber where opaque water cascaded over a thirty-foot fall, ending in a small clear pool below.

Rand pointed to a narrow, smooth-edged rock shelf near his feet. It forced them to move in a single file. "Be careful. It is wet and slippery," he said in a low tone. "I hate this cursed darkness. This place is meant for bats, snakes, and lizards, not us." He twitched unhappily.

Aurora rested a light hand on his shoulder for guidance and comfort. "At least it's not blood this time. Plus, I am *not* looking down."

Thirty paces passed beneath them the ledge widened, allowing them to walk alongside one another again as they traveled along the lake's dark edge. Aurora stopped as if pulled against her will, kneeling by the black water, which glistened ominously against the flickering torches. She leaned to inspect the still surface, stretching a hand outward, preparing to dip into the colorless liquid. Her fingers paused a mere inch from breaking its depths when Rand appeared by her side to lightly take her wrist.

"I wouldn't do that," he whispered. "The water seems unnatural, like everything else here." He pointed to his ear, then overhead as their gazes turned upward. Subconsciously, he clutched the amulet around his neck. "Listen and look around."

Scratching and scraping surrounded them, reminding Rand of his bedroom at night. He raised his arm and gave two sharp waves of his torch. Aurora followed suit. Too late, they realized their mistake. Here, in their comforting darkness, the creatures remained still and observant. But within the aura of the passing fire, their world transformed into unnerving anger.

Gradually, as the teen's sight adjusted, movement in the dark became clearer. Numerous shapes skittered atop the smooth stone. Red and yellow eyes with vertical slits stared at them like the glow of shining garnet or topaz gems embedded in rock. The ceiling curved near the fall's topmost portion, and reflections from the shifting, glowing orbs spoke to the cavern's deceiving magnitude. Oddly, the scene reminded Rand of watching flickering fireflies at night, though the accompanying emotions were anything but peaceful.

Aurora stiffened and pushed her back against the wall, refusing to move. But fear had driven blood into Rand's heart at a frantic pace. Seizing her hand, he pushed a finger to his lips before leading her to a rough outcropping of stone. He scanned about once more.

Hope sprang into his heart, for on the far side of the lake lay an expansive stone set of stairs, though neither end could be seen through the gloom since colors, aside from grey or black, lay mute around them. Thankfully, a path led them around its circumference.

Only the sputtering orange torchlight lent comfort as they entered the massive chamber. All the while, Rand continued to pray to the gods the creatures would not attack. Uncertain how he and Aurora had gotten this far without being assaulted, he counted his blessings but had no time to ponder an answer. They were safe in this moment, and that was all that mattered, save for a method of escape.

Their situation worsened as the search continued. Reaching the stairs proved harder than imagined as they fumbled in the weak orange glow. Many terrible writhing limbs reached for them through the darkness, grabbing and seizing any bit they could. Aurora swatted at them with her flame, causing painful squeals to erupt from the thick murkiness.

Rand stabbed here and there with his blade. Ghastly screeches arose while dark blood spilled onto the stone as he slashed and hewed. Urging Aurora forward, he broke into a run as smells of decaying corpses filled the air. The young man did not wish to know where the bones had come from or what manner of animal they once belonged to. Many were clearly human, evidenced by the partial skulls and pieces of skeletons scattered about.

Then, a terribly shrill sound erupted from Aurora's throat. Her outcry was unlike anything he had ever heard. He quivered at the awful sound as he spun to face her. She pointed her torch ahead.

Rand turned to find Clarissa's eyes staring back as if she stood ready to hug him. In a twisted moment, one pushing him nearer to the brink of insanity, he fathomed her head neatly placed on a rock ledge, her stare forever pointed up as if attempting to stargaze through the depths of her tomb.

Like the caretaker, her fragments had been strewn about like hideous decorations. A leg here, an arm there. Tears filled his eyes and slowly ran down his cheek. Behind him, Aurora's wails echoed off the surrounding rock, accompanied by the onrushing scuttle of beastly creatures.

The sound of their pursuers drove Rand out of sorrow. This was no time for crying. Grieving could come later. Tearing his eyes from the awful sight, he ran ahead with Aurora's hand in his own.

The boy continued to puzzle over why they had not become a meal yet. Did these creatures enjoy the chase? Perhaps they took cruel pleasure in human terror by remaining just out of reach while squalling and making unearthly noises as they gave pursuit. The monstrous things seemed to be toying with their prey. Perhaps, he thought, they were afraid, but of what he knew not. He quickly discarded that idea.

Then, beyond all likelihood, Aurora's unusually raspy voice brought more hope. "The air feels warmer. There must be a way out. Look, up ahead, a light."

"We're almost to the stairs," he confirmed before falling to his knees as both feet tangled in loose bones and whitened skulls. He sprang up quickly with an agonized expression. Blood flowed from an open gash on his palm. Scowling at his luck, he dashed on as his feet moved mechanically, never slowing. Wrapping the wound with a kerchief as best he could while jostling along, he continued.

The hateful orbed eyes followed along the walls, floor, and ceiling. Possibilities for escape were rapidly dwindling. Rand felt heated anger rise in him. He was tired of feeling scared and running. In an instant, he skidded to a stop, pulled back his shoulders, and raised himself to his full height, bracing both feet as a wellspring of bravery or foolishness exploded within him.

"Get on with it!" he yelled. The torch glowed in one hand, and the gleaming knife flashed in the other. "I will be chased no longer. Come, try and take me as you have taken the others." His amulet swayed against his shirt with each movement, reflecting in the dancing flame. Its shining surface threw brilliant rays of light outward.

Several creatures backed away while shielding their faces. Others closed in, then hesitated unexpectedly. Again, Rand tried to comprehend their actions. He recalled stories of vampires reacting similarly to mirrors or crosses, but he carried no such things, and these beings were assuredly not legends, tales, or vampires.

Suddenly, Aurora's hand closed around his collar and jerked him down the passage. "What are you doing? This is no time for heroics. Run, you idiot!"

Plodding ahead, madness quickly blazed into possibilities, swelling in their chests as they neared the stairs. Relentlessly, they went onward, yet Aurora's pace began to slow. Rand's did, too.

Finally, they reached the stairs. Upward they went as the horrid things gave chase, their pointed claws tapping the rock with a terrible, vexing rhythm. Some made a barely perceptible squelch—the sound a giant amphibian would produce. Neither Rand nor Aurora could spare the mental space or time to laugh at it.

Ultimately, they reached the end only to find a sealed door.

Hope melted into panic, then despair. Both torches clattered to the ground as Rand and Aurora pounded, pushed, clawed, and dashed themselves against the hard rock to no avail. The uncaring rectangle refused to budge as the creatures drew ever nearer.

Rand pressed as close as he could, running his hands over every crevice of the door in search of a hidden lever, knob, or button. It was not meant to be. Still closer, the creatures came, their repugnant glowing orbs widening in anticipation with each step. Sounds of their gnashing teeth and persistent claws clicking thundered in the boy's head, overtaking nearly all else.

After flattening his palms against the door in despair, Rand faced Aurora to hug her a final time. "I'm so sorry. I never thought our lives would end this way."

She smiled thinly through tears. "It's not your fault. But I am not going to die without a fight. I'm taking as many of them with me as I can." Bending down, she grasped her still-flickering torch and shifted her stance.

As she did, a loud clank resounded within the chamber. Rand's head jerked up, seeing her slightly elevated heel. Aurora accidentally stumbled on a small foot switch in a sheer stroke of good fortune. The door popped ajar. They bolted through the opening to thrust themselves back against it, finding great comfort in the resounding clinking sound as the passage resecured itself.

On the main floor again, the two squinted, raising their forearms to shield their eyes. After emerging from utter darkness, the greying light of evening was painful, but there was little time to adjust. They dashed through the halls, skidding around marbled corners toward the main entrance. Aurora threw her torch aside as Rand yanked open the heavy door, and together, they sprinted out onto the castle grounds.

Rand dared a glance to the west. The sun was descending. Would they make it home before the creatures, shrouded by darkness, released themselves? It was the night that gave them the power to frighten, hunt, and kill.

They ran for the winding wooded path leading to town until they could no longer maintain the frantic pace. Aurora slowed as they passed into long shadows beneath the tall trees, then halted for breath.

"Hold on! What is that?" she asked, staring at the dim light radiating from atop Rand's shirt.

Rand never looked down. Confused, he raised a shoulder. "What?"

She pointed. "Your necklace glowing? Why is it doing that?"

He raised the amulet before him as the sculpted lines slowly faded. "You know I've worn this for years. My grandparents gave it to me. They said it would . . ." He paused in thought as his mind worked at a feverish pace.

"Would what? Finish the thought," grumbled Aurora.

"It would keep me safe against beasts and creatures of the night. I've told you I always had trouble sleeping. I thought it was their way to pacify me so I could rest."

"Apparently not," she argued. "Do you think your grandparents saw these beasts? Were they keeping you from harm with some kind of weird magic?"

Rand shrugged. "I'll never know now. They disappeared years ago." Another curse escaped his lips. "How could I have not put this together?" He slapped his forehead. "After they gave it to me, they vanished. Mom and Dad didn't say where they went, only that Grammy and Gramps moved away."

"Holy crap!" Aurora's eyes bugged. "Do you think they sacrificed themselves to keep you safe?"

Rand hoisted his pack higher. "I wouldn't know why. I'm not special. Why not keep it for themselves? Why give it to me?"

"Maybe they knew their time was ending and wanted to protect the future generations. It is lovely, yet really sad, too," she replied before wiping a tear from her cheek.

The dissipating chaos behind them, Rand's face brightened. "I have an idea. We can be a team, like Holmes and Watson. Only instead of solving crime, we'll hunt monsters!"

"I wasn't supposed to grow up killing nightmares for a living," complained Aurora, crossing her arms defiantly as she began to walk. She quickly perked up. "But we do make a good team, Watson."

He frowned. "I wanted to be Holmes."

"Stop whining," she said, shoving his shoulder.

Rand nodded and took her hand. "We can help rid innocent people, kids especially, of the things that come in the darkness."

"Great idea, but who will protect us?" she asked.

Another shrug. "I'm guessing the amulet will do that part. If not, we can figure that out later. Remember, fear can only be conquered by facing it. So, into the darkness, we'll go."

Dusk faded to a star-filled night sky as the pair reached Rand's home. They proceeded upstairs, where Aurora spent the night on the soft bed with the young man lying next to her for protection.

Though exhausted, Rand would not sleep well that night. His mind was filled with questions concerning the nameless things lurking in shadowed places, ones finding solace in making their unspeakable homes within the darkness we fear.

EHRE DEINEN VATER (HONOR THY FATHER)

The room's center held another unmistakably dead woman, evidenced by the winding trail of blood draining from her neck. The viscous crimson liquid dribbled from the table onto the cold stone floor with a slow, perceptible splat.

Things were not supposed to be like this. Aaron dreamed of a normal life, not one of a killer. And though he never participated in the actual murders, the guilt of knowing and sharing in the acts, regardless of the degree, sat heavily upon his mind and heart. How long, he wondered, could he stand to witness them before insanity took him?

The echo of a solid door closing, followed by steady footfalls, brought him into the present. His father, a wealthy, remarkably unassuming man, shuffled down the stairs. Fashionably dressed and well groomed, he removed his coat and vest, then grabbed a scalpel.

Aaron remained hidden in the shadows, stiffened by incomprehensible horror. He clamped a hand over his mouth to stifle a scream. His gaze unwillingly settled on the naked corpse. For a moment, he hoped his father had forgotten him, but his hopes were soon dashed as the man paused to glance around.

"Dear boy, where are you? I am home from work. Come help your papa. There is work to do."

Aaron shuddered at the sound of his father's graveled voice. As they had for years, thoughts of leaving home weaved an intricate web in the young man's mind. However, his father was a respected, well-connected fellow. Attempting to avoid his evil influence, especially in this or any nearby town, would be impossible.

"Coming, Father," called Aaron, answering despite himself. Hesitantly, he moved toward the opposite side of the table, never looking at the once beautiful woman as he approached. Summoning every ounce of courage in his thin body, he confronted his father as best he could. "I . . . I . . . I thought we could stop this for a while and—" he began.

Laughter drowned out his words. "What has come over you, boy? There is endless evil to purge from this world, and it is our job to see that task through. You have been chosen to fulfill His purpose." The grim man's eyes went to the ceiling in reverence or prayer.

Aaron's timidness evaporated. It was the same speech and ridiculous notion his father always purported. He tightened his fist beneath the table, seething inside. Discontent rose in his heart and had to be voiced, regardless of the fact he would certainly be beaten for speaking out.

"Why did she deserve to die?" Finding the nerve to gently hold the cold woman's shoulder, he hoped she could somehow feel his remorse and pity. Perhaps she would even forgive him if her spirit—if there was indeed such a thing—could see him from high above.

"Because she wears the mark! Can you not see it?" cried his father, waving the gleaming blade about. "She is a spawn of hell. Daughter of the devil himself. Another strumpet of Satan." He pointed to her forehead with a sense of fervor. "Do you not plainly see the sign?"

Aaron spared a quick glance toward the corpse. There was no mark or sign. There never was. "What about him?" The young man pushed his chin toward a dismembered carcass on the nearest cart, then quickly looked away as the sight conjured horrendous images of a slaughterhouse. The thought turned his stomach.

"Did he have the mark, too?" he asked with unmistakable sarcasm. "Or did he simply spit on the sidewalk? Maybe he looked at a woman in a lustful way. Did the devil make him do that, too!" The boy leaned on the table's edge, his voice returning to its usual calm sound. "There is no devil, no mark, and nothing is wrong with these people other than you murdered them."

His father, Reinhold, dropped the blade to slam both palms on the table. "Damn you, boy, do not question me. He was an immoral heathen who kept a mistress—a slut—at his beck and call. Sinner, I say! God tasked me to cleanse him."

Aaron scoffed, buoyed by his growing resistance. "God! How ridiculous. There's no such thing. You are imagining these people bearing some evil mark. Even worse, you believe a non-existent deity is speaking to you. Madness! Father, you need help. We have plenty of money for you to seek a good doctor."

With surprising speed, Reinhold rounded the table's length, grabbing his son's shirt to pull him close. "God speaks to me, damn you!" He slapped his son's face twice, then pointed to the butchered man. "Now, take that scum to the furnace and burn him, as it should be, for flames will be his home for eternity! Cleanse him!"

Quickly composing himself, Reinhold smoothed Aaron's shirt nicely. "Never question my faith again, or perhaps one day you will join the non-believers, those *He* has marked for hell. It is unfathomable my own son dares speak blasphemy!" Pointing another stiff finger toward the door, he scowled. "I will tolerate your insolence no longer. Go! This wretched woman shall be your task once you return." Seizing the nearest scalpel, he jammed into her chest, leaving it protruding there.

He backed away and spread his arms wide, a malicious grin curving his lips. "Tonight, we will find another sinner, and your duty will be to carry out God's will. It is time for you to serve your savior."

The gleeful finality of his declaration silenced Aaron. Terrified beyond words at the thought of killing, the young man made his way to a different table. He loaded the bloody parts atop a wheeled cart as notions of cold-blooded murder haunted him, creeping into his bones like a parasite. With a forceful shove, he moved the contraption toward the doors and disappeared behind them as they swung closed.

Inside the boiler room, he wept freely, tears slipping down his cheeks to splash onto the bloody limbs. Inner remorse for the blameless souls was nearly unbearable. The feeling drained his resolve to the point he once considered ending his life. But that would not stop his father's murder spree. So onward, he went from fear alone, always keeping the spark of hope alive that things would somehow change.

He opened the heavy cast iron furnace doors and tossed the human remains into the dancing flames. The orange blaze engulfed each piece without care. The smell and heat were awful, yet Aaron persisted. His own life hinged on finishing this act of desecration.

Working at feverish speed, his mind sought a plan to avoid this evening's killing. Once the deed was done, he would be forced to return to the lab with his dead trophy to violate the woman's body with a knife and saw. Under his father's watchful eye, the young man would dissect her remains like some twisted experiment.

Without warning, bile rose in his throat. Grasping both knees, he vomited with force—one more thing he would need to clean up and dispose of, he thought. Wiping his face on his sleeve, he washed down the table, broomed the floor clean by pushing the blood and smaller pieces into the drain, then wheeled the empty cart back to the laboratory.

"Well done, my boy," said Reinhold, clapping lightly in patronizing fashion. "Come, now it is your turn. Complete this job." Retrieving a sizeable knife, he held it out and waited.

Aaron extended a shaking hand and took the blade but remembered very little after that moment as his father directed him through the proper techniques of skillfully ravaging a human body, all in the name of his ridiculous god. Cold flesh opened with each cut, slice, or hack. Organs dangled from the table's edge. Aaron saw it all through unfocused eyes and a blank mind. Edging toward a solid mixture of tears and irrationality, the young man mindlessly performed the task until, at last, his torment was complete.

Reinhold warmly embraced his son. "Excellent, son. You performed wonderfully!" he said happily. "You have the hands of a surgeon." The man's demeanor changed as he wiped his hands clean, the usual glower eclipsing his smile. "Now, put her in the furnace, then prepare for tonight. After dinner, we shall begin our latest quest. Do you understand?"

Nodding mutely, Aaron loaded the cart once more. As earlier, he finished the job, but not before more tears and vomit forced their way free from his body. To worsen his distress, the dead woman's voice wailed and moaned as he worked, echoing within the cold walls before settling in his ears, spreading an unnatural chill through his body. Her face appeared next, floating before his eyes as if pleading from the beyond to have her life returned—the one his father had taken without just cause.

Both eyes were absent from her deathly pale face. Only empty, blackened sockets stared outward. Panicking as she floated closer, Aaron threw both arms over his eyes and reeled, crashing into the cart tipping it over with a loud clatter. The noise drowned out her ghastly sounds. As her visage and voice faded, he heaved a long sigh, relieved her dreadful vengeance never arrived. He dabbed his sweating forehead with a kerchief, convincing himself the dead could not reach out, let alone do harm.

Once the horror subsided, he collected himself before trudging to his room, hoping tonight would never come.

What does one wear to commit murder? Aaron deliberated on the distasteful question, the only thought that could preoccupy him with his upcoming task. He chose a patched pair of trousers, a frayed shirt, and old boots. If they were ruined by blood, he could always burn them.

Moving to the window, he stared into the street, watching the passersby. He called them 'normies'—just ordinary, average, non-descript folks, ones never looked at twice by others. Which one of them would be their victim tonight? He saw a heavy woman, looking remarkably similar to the dog she was walking, going about her day oblivious to his watchful stare. A tall, stout man carried his happy daughter upon his broad shoulders. She giggled and waved at anyone who looked their way. To his right, a thick wooden park bench held an older couple sitting together as they tossed seeds to the cooing pigeons converged at their feet.

"I can't do it," Aaron said defiantly. "I am not a killer. These people have done nothing to me." He pounded his fist on the windowsill. "No! I am telling him I will have no part in his acts of madness."

With a soft sound, an orange tabby cat leaped upon the sill, rubbing its head against Aaron's cheek as he spoke. Her purring began immediately as the young man stroked the feline's back and gently ran his hand up her tail. With his mother murdered by his father's hands after insisting he saw the mark upon her, the cat named Lovey was the only female in Aaron's life. At least, the only one still living.

"Father has gone mad, and I can't stop him," he sighed. "He won't listen to logic." Lovey meowed a response and rubbed her forehead against his nose.

Aaron smiled as he softly scuffed her ears, but his tiny bit of happiness melted when a sudden shadow passed over the room. The sun had fallen from the evening sky. The horrendous feelings bubbled to the surface as his next inconceivable steps edged closer.

"I should summon a constable. But who would believe I had nothing to do with any of this," he asked softly. Another meow and nose rub were Lovey's responses. "Father may be a monster, but what would I do without him? I have no job, and both parents would be gone." His left eye twitched with an anxious reflex.

Rising to fill Lovey's food and water bowls, he glanced out the window again. Pale dusk was settling over the dirty city. Mere minutes remained before Aaron would become the monstrosity he feared most—death. Not just any version of death, but one who carefully chose, stalked, and preyed upon innocents. He wiped his sweaty palms on his trouser thighs.

Sick revulsion tightened his throat as Reinhold's weight made the floorboards creak. The sound of his footsteps cemented the reality. Now, there was no shaking the belief that Papa would want his son to become a beast, a brutally cold, calculating animal of the night.

With a last dejected look into the depths of blackening night, the boy waited, shivering against the chill in his heart. Finally, the dreaded knock on the door came. The moment Aaron feared most had arrived.

"Meet downstairs in five minutes. Do *not* be late," grumbled Reinhold.

"Yes, Papa," he answered before listening attentively as his father strode the hall's length to descend the creaking stairs in his usual heavy, steady gait.

Aaron paced feverishly, his mind rattling, yet no viable avoidance plan came. Covering the knife and cudgel hanging from his belt with a light coat, he opened his door, kissed Lovey's head in farewell, and headed toward the front door.

Reinhold stood waiting, looking pleased his son would be his accomplice for their first wicked adventure as a team.

Like ghosts, the two crossed the threshold and slipped unseen into deep night. Streetlamps lit their way, but there were enough unlit alleys and shadowed corners to spring from should they need to, Aaron thought in despair. Father had chosen not to use their motor, which meant the victim would need to be carried to the laboratory. He hoped it was not a far distance. It would prolong his nightmare even longer.

As time passed unnoticed, Aaron listened to his father grumble under his breath as he reasoned his way to the perfect victim. The man methodically searched for a sign only he saw, holding no concern for height, weight, beauty, or other trivial factors. Papa wanted sinners. Plain and simple. Those he believed his God cursed.

Aaron, disgusted by the whole affair, thought of nothing more than going home. Conversely, Reinhold searched on as they roamed through the gloomy streets, refusing to give up. Thankfully, to Aaron, none seemed to catch the man's fancy this evening.

However, a small-statured girl crossed their path near the end of their long, disappointing walk home alone. Reinhold eased into the shadows, quickly guiding his son to his side. He pressed a finger to his lips.

"She will do fine. Take her, now. She bears the mark," he whispered. "It blazes like fire. Look!" He pushed his chin in her direction.

"But Father, she's so young," argued Aaron.

"Do as I say," retorted Reinhold, seizing his son's arm above the elbow and squeezing until he whimpered.

Physically and mentally exhausted, turmoil gripped Aaron's mind. Repeatedly, he asked himself why this young woman should die. No answer came. Beyond all semblance of doubt or reason, his father was unstable. Yet, what recourse did he possess to banish the iniquity from his father's soul? Again, leaving home came to mind, but that would leave Reinhold to his own devices—none of which were kind. Even now, his son could barely contain the murderer. If Aaron suddenly vanished, Reinhold could delve into a murderous spree unlike any seen before.

Reinhold squeezed his son's arm again, then pointed toward the approaching victim. "Now, boy, now! Kill her quickly," he hissed, his eyes glowing like streetlamps, highlighting his frenzied state.

Aaron reached into his coat, felt the knife handle, and hung his head in shame. Gathering resolve, he sprang from the night's deep shadows to rap the woman's head with the cudgel. She dropped in an instant, piling up on the sidewalk, unconscious. He thanked his gods for giving him the presence of mind to bring the weapon to delay the kill somehow.

"You fool!" droned Reinhold through gritted teeth. "You were supposed to kill her."

The young man's mind whirled for a reasonable excuse. "We'll take her back to the house so I may have more time with her. I will make her confess her sins. I did it for you, papa," he improvised beneath his father's scrutinous glare. For good measure, he added another placating thought. "That way, you can teach me even more."

Light of a different kind illuminated Reinhold's eyes. Again, he clasped a surprisingly strong hand on the boy's shoulder. "Right, you are! Excellent idea." His gaze covered the girl. "Delightful! Help me carry her. Quickly now."

———————

As the sun rose, shining dim light through the windows high above, Aaron rose and stretched to full height within the laboratory. He'd slept well, or as well as he could underneath the circumstances, which were somewhat improved. At least the girl was still alive. His father had been too tired to carry out their awful plans the previous night, especially once he began drinking. He had staggered to bed, saying the girl could be dealt with during morning's light.

Aaron sat on the small bed in the dank corner near the swinging doors, primarily considering his predicament and watching his future victim's firm breasts rise and fall with each steady breath. His eyes covered her frame. Except for a pair of dainty undergarments, she was naked and exposed. It seemed demoralizing to her person, so Aaron moved to slide a sheet to her neck, covering her near nakedness. She barely stirred.

Breathing deeply to draw in her scent, he smiled. The lavender aroma resembled one his mother had worn, but he quickly tried to banish the memory. Connecting the two would only make the upcoming task even more difficult.

Aaron had never felt a woman's soft, warm flesh, save for gentle touches on his cheeks from his mother years ago. He admired the unconscious girl's beauty since, other than corpses, he had no life experience with the opposite sex. His father had bought him a whore once, but the meeting turned to failure when Aaron was too nervous to perform. Reinhold chastised and beat him for his lack of manliness and desire.

Here and now, during the night, while the girl lay insensible and oblivious to his prodding, he ran both hands over her softly muscled legs and arms, stroked her hair, and admired the angles of her high cheeks, rounded chin, and perfectly shaped nose. She looked more lovely than any vision he could have imagined. He drew back, suddenly concerned his actions were rather odd or perverse. How could he explain his burning desire to feel a woman's soft embrace or kiss? It is natural, is it not, he wondered.

As he turned to cleaning the death room, as he called it, moans and whimpers arose from the girl. Aaron stopped sweeping, wondering if he should go to her, then dismissed it. He might only make her panic further. But just as he resumed his tidying, screams, and shrieks broke the air. Then came the unmistakable sound of shaking leather restraints and sobbing.

Aaron ran to her side, waving both hands before patting her forearm in hopes of comforting her somehow. "Stop! You must stop. Father will be home from work soon. He cannot know you're awake."

"Why am I here? Who are you? Please, let me go, I beg you." She squirmed again, but her efforts were useless against her bonds. "I have money. A lot of it, too. I'll give it all to you. Don't hurt me."

Inexplicably, without leaving out a single detail, Aaron told his captive everything, as if confessing to a priest before being put to death. The relief of his declaration rushed over him, unplanned but welcomed. The sensation weakened his knees yet lifted his mental burden all the while.

"How old are you? What's your name?" he asked.

"Sixteen. I'm Lily," she answered before pleading once more. "Please don't hurt me. I've done nothing to you." Her head lifted as she squirmed once more. She relaxed her struggles, fathoming defeat. With deliberation, her gaze traversed the length of Aaron's body. "What about you? How old? What's your name? I bet it's strong, just like you."

He blushed. "Seventeen." He touched his chest. "I'm Aaron." Unable to meet her eyes any longer, he toyed with his shirt sleeve.

"Fetch my clothes before it's too late. Please, Aaron, please." Her eyes widened when he didn't move. "Come with me. We can be gone before your father gets home. I know places where we can be safe. You don't want to hurt me, I can tell."

The idea of a happy future was everything he wished for. Aaron flushed with momentary joy, imagining an uninhibited life free of Papa's madness. Seconds later, he snorted as doubts and fears drowned out hopes of starting anew. He shook his head.

"He would find me, then kill me, just as he promised."

It was then footsteps resounded overhead. Aaron's eyes widened as they went to the ceiling. Terror etched on his face.

"He's home. He'll kill us both." He ran to the back room, fetched Lily's clothes, then returned to hurriedly free her from the restraints. "Get dressed. You have to leave . . . now!" He swept an arm toward the basement's exit door.

"What about you?" she pressed, wobbling on one leg as she jammed her other limb through her pants. "Come with me. We can go to the constabulary."

Before Aaron could answer, familiar footfalls resonated from the first floor seconds before the laboratory door creaked open. Reinhold began descending the winding stone stairs, his boots clacking softly as he drew closer.

The young man's hasty plan was falling apart. Unnerved, he seized Lily's wrist and held a finger to his mouth, pursing his lips for quiet. He hurried her down a small hallway, jerked open a door, then pushed her inside.

"I'll be back for you soon. I promise. Just be patient . . . and perfectly quiet." He closed her in without waiting for a reply, then rushed back to the laboratory to take up a knife. Hesitating an instant to gather a dose of valor, he ran the steel across his forehead and wrist with quick movements, stifling a shriek as the flesh opened.

This ruse has to convince Father. He cast himself on the floor as blood ran down his cheek to stain his shoulder. His wrist formed a growing crimson pool near his extended arm. It took all he had to not move, but oddly enough, it became easier the longer he lay in wait. Nightmarish worry blurred both pain and time.

From his vantage, through partially closed eyelids, he watched Reinhold's feet reach the final step to touch the floor. Silence. Then, in a sudden, panicked flurry of activity, the man dashed about the room.

"Where is she!" he cried repeatedly. "No! She can't be gone!" He kicked the table over and ran his arm across a workbench, wiping it clean of several beakers and instruments. Aaron saw his father's feet turn toward him and then heard a choked gasp. Rapid footsteps closed the distance, and strong arms encircled him, raising his torso halfway up against his father's chest. "Son, what happened? Speak. Can you hear me?"

Aaron faked drowsiness, whimpering a convincing sound as his father shook him to supposed consciousness. Wiping blood from his face, the young man sat bolt upright, feigning shock and fear. His fresh wounds were smarting, but he never let on.

"Damn it, boy, where is the girl!" cried Reinhold, shaking and jerking his son's shoulders. "We must find her."

"Father, calm down. She has likely been gone for hours. We'll never find her. I'm sorry," lied Aaron, careful not to allow his wandering eyes to inadvertently give the girl's location away. Father was very keen that way. He could detect deception with little effort.

"How!" he shouted. "How did she escape? You bloody fool. You were to kill her last night. Idiot!"

While Aaron invented reasons why he did not follow orders, Reinhold's face flushed with anger. His arm lashed out, his fist catching Aaron's head, knocking him back to the floor.

"Worthless buffoon! You've made a mess of everything! We'll be discovered now. You are supposed to honor thy own father and do His bidding, not turn our lives upside down!"

Grimacing at his injuries and the painful blow, Aaron rose slowly. Father, still ranting, turned about in circles near the table, spittle flying from his mouth, oblivious to his son rising to full height behind him.

Rubbing his cheek and jaw where he had been struck, Aaron's eyes narrowed. He jerked the knife free from its hiding place and paused. A step forward, then a falter. His grip tightened. *Now*, he told himself. There would be no other time. His feet slapped the cold stone as he lunged at his father, swinging the blade with speed and precision.

Reinhold cried out as the sharpened steel crossed his chest. The gash bled heavily as he stumbled to the table's edge, shocked into a wordless state. But within a moment's breath, he threw himself forward, sending another fist to the side of his son's head. The boy collapsed in a barely conscious heap, unable to rise as his father pounced, straddling his body and pummeling him repeatedly.

Aaron closed his eyes, too dazed to resist or defend himself, knowing Lily likely watched in terror from the partially opened closet door, her hand affixed over her mouth. He wondered if he would be beaten to death before her eyes. He considered what type of strange fate reversal that would be as blackness closed in.

Then, thoughts of his mother flooded his mind. Her peaceful, beautiful image brought a blissful numbness as his father continued his assault. Would he soon join her, he wondered. Undoubtedly, she was not spending eternity in hell with the other sinners as father proclaimed.

Suddenly, Aaron heard a rush of footsteps coupled with a shuffling commotion. The noises around him were followed by a disgusting gurgling sound. A warm, sticky liquid sprayed his face, yanking him from his dream. He grimaced at the feel. Confused, his eyes opened to find a wooden knife handle protruding from his father's neck, the blade tip poking out the opposite side.

Reinhold's arm was extended as if begging for help as his empty stare met Aaron's eyes. Blood fountained from the wound as he wobbled horribly before careening toward his son. Aaron flinched, bracing for the impact, but it never came.

Like a dream, Lily was suddenly there to push the dead body onto the floor. She pulled Aaron to his feet.

"Are you okay?" she asked, running a hand over the gash on his forehead. She retrieved a towel and swabbed the blood away. Her body relaxed at the sight of the shallow cuts. His lips and nose still bled from the beating. One eye was already swelling shut.

He nodded. "I'm fine. You saved my life. I will owe you forever. But now, I need your help, please."

Lily's next question dissipated as the thuds of the young man's kicks to Reinhold's body resounded beside her. The pent-up rage and frustration could no longer be contained.

Once he was done, the pair struggled to lift his father's corpse onto the table. Aaron strapped on an apron and took up a saw.

Lily looked horrified. "What are you doing?"

"Getting rid of evidence . . . like he had made me do for years." His wild eyes settled on his tormentor's body. Pulling the blade free, he smiled. "I have been liberated. But don't worry," he added, speaking more to the corpse than to the living girl next to him, "I will do my duty and honor thy father." He stared into the lifeless blue eyes of his papa. "You will join the souls of all those you have murdered. I hope they honor you, too. Perhaps they can provide a bit of eternal torture in the place you are certainly going, beloved father. That is my gift to you."

He systematically butchered the corpse until, just as Reinhold had shown him, only neat pieces lay before him. Piling the portions onto the cart, as he had done many times before, he headed for the furnace. Lily trailed after him. The sounds of her retching faded from sense as he tossed one armful after another into the hungry flames. He could not rid himself of the evil fast enough.

Afterward, the duo cleaned the laboratory in fast order. Aaron was quite used to straightening the mess, while Lily struggled initially.

"I still can't believe this happened. Please tell me it's a dream. Please," she pleaded.

Aaron shook his head. "I wish it was." He paused to look squarely at her. "Can you keep this mess a secret, or should I run now?"

Lily stepped closer. "Aaron, I'm involved, too. I have no intention of telling anyone I killed a man—no matter the circumstances." As the deed sunk deeper into her consciousness, she rubbed her face and spoke softly. "We've just *killed* someone."

"We stopped a killer—a mass murderer," he corrected. "In the end, he got what he deserved. Besides, I did my duty and honored him by sending him to the hell he believes in."

Some days later, a bumbling pair of constables arrived to investigate reports of Reinhold bafflingly missing work. They went away with no more answers than before. Aaron lied, of course, simply telling them his father left town on a business trip, and he had no idea how long Reinhold would be away or even where he had gone.

As days passed without a sign of the missing man, Aaron remained proud and relieved that the local killings had stopped. Only Lily and he knew the truth of the gruesome events within the depths of the cold laboratory walls. They took comfort in knowing Reinhold would never return to kill again.

Even the mood around town lightened once the murders came to an end. People emerged from their homes more freely, especially at night. Happy voices could be heard through open windows, and smiling faces prevailed again.

Weeks later, with the abundance of his father's money at his fingertips, Aaron crafted a carved wooden plaque to hang above his house door. Simple in design, the phrase reminded him each day of his endured horror and revulsion felt within the walls of his home. It read only three words—Honor Thy Father.

TROUBLE IN BALNORVIA

F all had arrived. No matter the direction I looked, endless miles of nature's magnificence filled my vision. The day could not have been more wonderful. Colorful, rolling mountains decorated my present path as the horses trotted along contentedly, the carriage proving little burden to my fine animals.

I ventured north after receiving an unexpected invitation from the Duke of Balnorvia. Our paths had intersected but once before—a social gathering, the purpose of which I barely recall. However, the man himself made a lasting impression. Daresay, I was shocked he remembered my name, let alone took the time to grace me with a personal summons.

Yet, I was giddy as a schoolboy to be on the road again. While the horses clopped along at a relaxed pace, following the wide dirt road as if they had been here before, my mind moved to the reason for the upcoming visit. The Duke, an attractive, intelligent, tall man with dark features, had pleaded for my arrival, saying villagers were randomly disappearing. No explanation for the dozen or so vanishings stood the test of logic. No bodies had been discovered, and no foul play was suspected. Still, they were missing all the same, so I could not, in good conscience, decline the visit.

The Duke, or Byron, as I have come to know him, had a throng of townsfolks pleading for a resolution to this mystery. Hence, the reason I was summoned. As a writer and seasoned investigator of unnatural events, it seems I remained on his mind since our lone encounter.

Naturally, I offered to help, especially after receiving generous compensation. I also hoped the sum would not overpay me, for in my experience, such cases generally involve silly, often overlooked remedies. Why, just last week, I had been hastily called to deal with a matter of eerie noises distressing an already frightened staff at a local inn.

To my credit, dismissing my ego entirely, I solved the case within minutes. After one walk-through of the inn, I determined the shrill sounds came from unsealed windows, allowing wind to whistle and moan from their deteriorated edgings. Another source of the fabled banshee's wail, as one hapless cook named them, was in fact a swirling breeze crossing over the stovepipe.

Of course, the event sparked a fantastic idea, which I promptly turned into a successful novel. With luck, perhaps this outing would yield comparable results. Though I never struggled for new ways to terrify people with my words, I could not pass up such an opportunity.

Here, I must beg forgiveness for my lacking manners. I have rambled on without any form of introduction. I am many things, as you may have guessed. I am a writer, seeker of mysteries, lover of knowledge, intellect, observer, wealthy aristocrat who does not follow the fold, and finally, alone in my quest to seek the truth, whatever it may be. My name is Gerrit van Egmond, son of Willem Gerritsz van Egmond, the renowned supernatural investigator.

———

The horses rested only once, but Balnorvia is no short distance away, so we hoped to reach the castle by nightfall. Shortly after dusk, I arrived in the village, expecting to see daily happenings in full view, but what met my tired eyes was quite the opposite. I observed no human life amongst the cobbled streets, brick shops, or wooden houses. The phrase 'ghost town' crossed my mind, and I liked it. I have written that down for future reference.

Ghosts are pure nonsense, of course. I say this only since no solid evidence exists, save only for entertaining tales from the mouths of fearful, superstitious fools. I have yet to witness an apparition or so-called spirit throughout my many years of investigating such things. That naturally discounts those who try to fool me with their claims. Ghosts are mere fables, though I try desperately to keep an open mind. To my account, I go on.

As the sky turned sallow, preparing for night to conquer day, I rounded a gentle corner on the tree-lined road. There, a clearly marked path leading to my destination revealed itself.

I traveled the winding path briefly, halting my carriage before the castle's entrance. A bleak-looking fellow quickly relieved me of my rig. He seemed strong and fit enough, though his cheek was heavily scarred, possibly from the last war. Polite, he nodded and bowed several times. Yet, his quirky movements made me pause to wonder if his mental faculties should be questioned, and I did not have to wait long to confirm my hypothesis.

The man was indeed a clod. While unloading my bags, he tripped on his unmoving feet and stumbled into me. Again, he bowed several times, tipped his hat, and continued without comment. Feeling sorrow for the man, I mentioned an extra silver would be his reward if my animals were looked after to the best of his ability. That brightened his vacant expression. I named him Ezra since every castle should have an odd sort of fellow to tend to the master and the structure itself. The name means 'help,' which I thought befitting.

Topping the wide stone stairs, I paused before the large wooden doors and studied the iron raven's head knocker. It was a beautiful likeness. I grasped the intricate object and tapped it against the striker. At once, the sound resonated deep within, spreading unnatural fear in my heart. The sensation made me falter. Though I could not, nor dare not, guess the source, it gripped me all the same. My premonitions are rarely incorrect or without merit, and this time, the feeling bothered me greatly. Was there something inside to be aware of?

Once the entry swung wide, another fellow—by appearances, the butler—allowed me entrance to the foyer. We exchanged names. His was Wilford. More pleasant and well-kept than Ezra, he showed me to my room, brought delectable food, and ensured a hot bath was drawn while assuring me that the Duke would greet me for an early breakfast. I did not question why Byron could not meet that night, but Wilford took it upon himself to say his lord was presently occupied. It hardly mattered, for that was just as well to my exhausted, travel-wearied mind. Bidding the butler a pleasant goodnight, I snuggled into bed and slept as soundly as I do in my own home, my fear gone now that I settled in.

———————

To my left, at the table's head, the Duke looked worn with worry, his face gray and lined with far more wrinkles than before. After reacquainting ourselves over our meal, Byron steered the conversation to the situation and reiterated his longing to be free of the nightmare he had unwillingly fallen into.

As usual, I asked if any recent events struck his mind, standing out as different from everyday affairs. Byron's only mention was an odd meteor shower of grand magnificence. During his account, he noted the sheer number of objects that had hurtled overhead. Dozens were spotted within a several-hour window. The event occurred some two weeks prior, near the exact time of the disappearances.

At this point, the subject of such an encounter temporarily erased all concerns over the disappearances. Some objects inevitably would have struck the Earth, and the sole motivation for my curiosity was to discover one. A piece of space rock falling into our laps would be invaluable for scientific study or sale. As Byron went on, further suggesting the happening was unrelated and led us no closer to the problem, I tried to hide my disappointment. However, I did document my desire to begin a new hunt once the disappearances were resolved.

As we dined, a breathless young lad arrived at the castle. Wilford led him in. The boy, Henry, a thin, short lad with brown hair and eyes, offered forth a note which Byron read.

The Duke scribbled a reply and returned the parchment, along with several coppers from his vest pocket. "Tell the constable we will be along directly," he added.

"As you wish, my lord," replied Henry. "Thank you, my lord."

The young man bowed, tucked the letter in his tunic, and then headed for the door with quick steps, vanishing from sight in moments. Fear seemed to drive his gait, though I saw no need for it. Something odd was at hand, but I could not say what.

Byron explained the message. Some missing villagers had been discovered. I had thought this news might spur some relief from the Duke, but it was not the case, perhaps because of the oddity that their condition was not yet disclosed. Still, the constable had pleaded for us to come at once.

Grabbing my frock coat and reaching for my pipe and tobacco inside its pocket, I discovered a scrap of parchment claiming the author of said writing had already viewed the bodies, stating horrible things had been imparted upon them. Each was rent, torn, and difficult to view. Ghastly was the word they used. Where had this mysterious note come from? I had not the time to search for its author. Possibly a prank, I thought as I followed Byron out. Standing near the carriage that would take us to the village was Ezra, the hapless fellow who had collided with me last night. Could he have slipped the note into my pocket? Time permitting, I would question him later.

———

We arrived at the village quickly, where the lead constable met us. He was a short, dour, fat man who seemed angry for being cheated out of the advantages of height. To ease his torment of knowing he could do nothing to improve his vertical situation, he turned to food, evidenced by the crumbs on his jacket and the unmistakable outline of a circular pastry in his coat pocket.

After polite introductions to learn our guide's name was Rupert, he led us to the morgue. My worst fears were taking shape. Before arrival in Balnorvia, I hoped death would not be involved. I was wrong. Yet, there could easily be a simple explanation for their demise. After all, men do horrendous things to one another, which could be such a case.

We descended the stairs into a cold room inside the drab stone building. As the constable led us to the tables, something was clearly wrong. The sheets covering the cadavers lay draped at odd angles as if disguising boxes of wood scraps beneath them. I concluded there was a mistake on the large man's part. How the constable did not mention this made me question his competency. Perhaps his slow wits came from pulling the cork once too often, and he had no idea what he was doing. Had his limited wits been dulled by drink or drugs? Though I observed no evidence of such behavior, it was simply an impression formed from his demeanor and the absurd lack of sharing information.

As the stiff white sheet was yanked free, I sucked in a quick breath, momentarily stunned by the gruesome scene.

The first corpse, if one could even name it so, lay in twisted fragments like mismatched pieces from many different puzzles. I moved closer, mentally retracting my previous thoughts concerning the prank. This affair was no such thing.

While I walked from one corpse to another with the Duke by my side, the constable offered much conjecture on how these poor folks came to be in this state. But I could not force myself to harken to his words. They were so close to stupidity. He driveled on about how wild animals—bears, boars, or the like—had committed this deed. Nothing could be further from the truth, and one only had to look upon the mutilated bodies for a moment to glean that understanding.

My theory was he simply wished the entire ordeal to vanish to not spoil his reputation, whatever that may be. It was hard to imagine he bore any prominence or good standing amongst the villagers, except for being dull-witted or turning his head when needed, if coins found their way into his pudgy palm.

Studying the shape and pattern of the wounds ruled out any wild animal. At least any with size enough to commit this atrocity. The lacerations resembled a mixture of a bear's claw coupled with colossal bite marks, far more extensive than I had ever seen.

This creature, or man, more likely, killed with wanton lust. No other valid explanation for such unjustifiable mutilations would stand the test of reason. Truthfully, as the mortician attempted to piece the bodies together, I remained flummoxed over the exact number of victims lying before me. It would take some hours to accurately solve the riddle.

By mid-afternoon, we had pooled our resources to surmise there were four distinct victims, leaving at least eight unaccounted for. With their slaughtered neighbors lying before us, hope for their survival was slim. Townsfolk would surely panic, I thought. Who could blame them? From this day forward, once word was leaked of this discovery, terror would fester in their hearts.

"Bloody hell, man, tell us what you think," crowed the constable.

My eyes went to the Duke. "Only the most depraved soul would take pleasure in slaughtering others so unmercifully," I said. "I suspect word of this deed shall spread like wildfire. There will be panic. Perhaps rightly so. Whoever committed these acts was beyond any depravity I have ever witnessed. That, my fine gentlemen, is a fact."

"B . . . b . . . but what about a bear or some such," stammered Rupert.

Gerrit ignored the comment. "My good man, I have seen enough. Please excuse us," I announced.

Byron and I excused ourselves to reenter the street, strolling through the village while discussing theories and facts. Many were ruled out, while some piqued my interest wholly.

As stated earlier, even to the untrained observer, excluding the buffoon of a constable, these deaths were no accident. No animal could have performed such atrocious acts. The question begging to be asked was, why? What purpose would be served by killing innocents in such a fashion? Terror? Revenge? Greed? None seemed likely for such violence.

For certain, no institutionalized mental patients had made a recent escape. The victims, at least to this point, had no apparent ties to one another, and the severity of the attack lent credence to more than one perpetrator. Even though a lone madman could do such a deed unimpeded by interruptions.

Thudding footfalls came from behind before Rupert appeared, puffing heavily as he trotted to catch us. I refuse to say he ran, for none would believe such an absurd tale. The fellow's undersized legs barely upheld his weight, let alone supported any type of running. Reaching our side, he slowed to a walk, seeming pleased with the pace as he gulped for air.

"My lord," he huffed to Byron. "What is the next step? What do you wish of me now?"

"If I may," I interjected, facing the breathless constable. "Please take us to the location where the bodies were found. I wish to examine the scene."

"At your service. I will fetch a carriage and return promptly," Rupert said, moving off. The huffing began again, redolent of a slow-moving steam train as he shuffled away.

Byron and I sat on the lip of a gurgling fountain within the town square. The sound of gently splashing water soothed me. As I took in the sights of the towering treed slopes, small shops, and homes below them, I developed empathy for these people. Their serene lives in the surrounding peaceful hills had been disrupted by most atrocious murders, and with several now discovered, news of the horrible methods of death would not long remain hidden.

Mere moments seemed to have passed before clopping horses drew my attention. Rupert arrived, expertly steering a coach through the gaggle of townsfolk to reach us. Byron and I exchanged a wry smile. We had discovered a use for the man—coach driver extraordinaire. Or so I would deem him.

———————

Fifteen minutes or so passed before we dismounted from our conveyance. For the second time since my arrival, disbelief gripped me. From our vantage point, a swatch of forest was missing, completely removed, to the bare Earth in some parts. We hurriedly crossed another fifty yards into a small valley to stop above an enormous fissure, the lip of which we perched upon to stare downward.

Inside a smoldering crater, a tremendous black sphere protruded from the soil. My heart pounded with nervous excitement. Factually, I had never seen any such material before. No human hands could have created something so flawless and magnificent. It gleamed in the sunlight, perfectly round and shining like a glass marble. Fragmented pieces of rock lay strewn over fifty paces as if thrust outward from the inside. A once protective outer shell, I mused, bending to eagerly scoop up several smaller pieces and place them in my pocket.

"By the gods," said the Duke. "Why was I not informed of this?"

"I was hoping to gather more details. But once a young lad walking his dog came across this mess, I knew it was too late," admitted Rupert. "As for the boy, he was warned not to be out and about during such times, but you know, children. And I've heard folks sayin' the dead ones . . . er, I mean, victims, came to gawk at the big hole and were never seen again . . . until now."

To my dismay, I had been so enthralled by the scientific marvel I had wholly ignored the awful scene around me. The abundance of blood, brain matter, bones, and torn clothing spread about was prominent on this bright, cloudless day. It appeared ravenous beasts had pulled those unfortunate people apart. However, Rupert's earlier story was absurd since we had no hard proof.

I assessed the bones first. Great gashes were present on each victim. Many bore bite marks akin to those poor souls in the morgue—wide, with many rows of teeth. A sizable shark's bite would be the closest image I could conjure. I hurriedly pulled a pencil and small notebook from my frock to sketch my observations.

"Why did you not bring either material or remains to the morgue?" I asked, perplexed.

Rupert raised a shoulder and reddened from embarrassment. "My helpers saw to this site since I was indisposed then. I assumed the dolts had carried out my orders."

"Indisposed at the local pub, I imagine," retorted the Duke. "It may be time for a new lead constable in our town, wouldn't you say, Rupert? Perchance, the young Stoddard boy would take your place. He is stout and quick-witted."

The heavy man stammered and toyed with his sleeve cuff like a scolded child. "M . . . m . . . my lord, he's but twenty-three years old. He knows nothing about the law. And, a bit of a braggart, as well. He's a bully to most folks. He's a fool."

I pitied the doltish man named Rupert and attempted to smooth things over for him. "Perhaps the constable has learned his lesson," I offered, though I held no faith in my own words. "Surely, his methods will improve now that the flaw has been brought to his attention." My eyes met his as he nodded vigorously, relief flooding his fleshy face.

"Right you are, sir! Count on me. I will make both of you proud," he answered, straightening his unclean uniform and hair, then thrusting his chest out.

Byron and I made brief eye contact, knowing the vow was empty. We dropped the subject.

"Do you believe the ones still unaccounted for could have witnessed this?" asked the Duke, stroking his groomed beard while deep in contemplation.

"Possibly." Rupert pointed east. "They live on the outskirts of town. Just there." He inclined his head to the side as thoughts formed. "Come to think of it, everyone between here and the village has disappeared. Like a straight line of sorts."

"You are just now connecting that piece?" I rose with a start. My current theories were pure conjecture, but the idea of marauding invaders hitting the weakest or most isolated first made perfect military sense. If that was the case, these beings were intelligent, organized, and vicious. "We should return to the village. I am convinced it is unsafe here. Pass the word none should draw near these woods until further notice."

Rupert balked at the prospect. "B . . . b . . . but, sir, this road is the only one from town. What will do for supplies and such?" he questioned.

"If you wish to stay alive a bit longer, heed my advice." I waved my two colleagues over and pointed to the overturned, soft ground. "What do you make of that?"

Both Byron and Rupert surveyed the claw-like indentations leading into the woods. They looked as confused as I felt. I could not leave without further investigation.

We took up the crooked trail, heading for the dismally dark forest, spreading out as we progressed. Within twenty yards of entering,

Rupert shrieked and pointed. Byron and I sprinted to his side for a sight I shall never forget, no matter if I was immortal.

Horrible to look upon, the creature was bipedal, four feet in height, with two thin legs supporting large, clawed feet. Thick, dark blue skin covered its small, muscular frame. Long arms hung from narrowed shoulders with five identical digits like its feet. Pointed ears protruded through holes on both sides of a small metallic helmet. A compact body spoke to the creature's ability to move quickly. Its garb was simple—a cloth material protruded beneath sheer, flexible armor, covering only the chest and back. A short, sheathed sword was mounted on its back, overtop the protective apparel. Its face was incredible, with a wide, gaping mouth filled with rows of pointed teeth. One eye stared back. The invader was cyclopic.

How this creature met its doom was impossible to say without further study.

Beside me, Rupert turned deathly pale and looked near retching. Byron grimaced but held a steadfast course. Meanwhile, I had more questions than answers. It appeared my previous assumptions were wholly incorrect. These murders were not the work of a lone, crazed lunatic or a gang of miscreants. These deaths could be a story from my novels.

We had stumbled across travelers from another world, even though I could not reasonably explain their origin. There could be no other logical deduction. How does one imagine such a tale reaching fruition? Before this day, despite believing we are not alone in the universe, I could not have foreseen finding such remarkable evidence to support such a theory.

"I shall bear this creature to the carriage," I said, scooping the small being up in my arms. Despite a vicious appearance, its skin was surprisingly smooth and soft. "We must preserve the body. What a spectacular find!"

"Wonderful idea, Gerrit," said Byron. "This creature could change many scientific minds as to their existence."

"I am *not* sitting near that thing," Rupert stated matter-of-factly, pushing his chin toward the alien. "It's downright peculiar. There's some queer goings-on, I tell you."

"Then you shall walk back to the village. For I will not leave a discovery of this nature lying here simply because you lack courage," I retorted firmly. "We will meet you at the inn. Farewell."

Rupert rubbed his bulging belly before finding his better sense. "Fine! But I won't like it. That thing is cursed."

"The word you are searching for is *dead*," I corrected. "Curses are for weak-minded fools. Let us move along. Hurry now."

––––––––

During the small hours of the night, our examination concluded. As we stepped outside for fresh air, I was never more pleased to see the sky. Overhead lay a cloudless canopy of blackness, save for the sliver of a waning crescent moon, our only natural illumination. It looked glorious but only partially soothed the turmoil I felt upon finishing the exam. I saw no visible wounds on the alien, nor could I explain its demise. Perhaps it was severely injured in the crash and simply expired as it attempted to seek shelter.

"Gerrit," began the Duke, "what shall we do?"

"Defend ourselves by any means necessary. I have pieced together another theory. If your story is accurate concerning the falling meteors, there could be dozens of these beings. I venture a guess some of those meteors were spacecraft."

Rupert laughed while holding his round belly. "Oh, sir, that's rich! And it surely does sound just plain ignorant."

"Then perhaps you can explain it to us without your dubious theories of bears, boars, or the like," said Byron, folding his arms across his chest in wait.

I interjected before the rotund man could start again and test our thinning patience. "We do not know if these creatures kill for food, defense, or sport. Nonetheless, we may be outnumbered, according to your own accounts."

"Defense," cried Rupert, placing both hands on his hips as he laughed again. "Are ya' totally daft, man? Who would hurt them?"

"Besides fleeing as fast as your small feet would carry you, what would you have done had you come across this being if it were alive?" I paused, waiting for Rupert's answer that would not come. "You would have tried to kill it, no?"

The constable shrugged. "M . . . m . . . maybe."

"Therefore, I restate my position." I pointed to the three of us in turn. "Humans may have been the aggressors here. These creatures may have meant no harm. Perhaps they landed from desperation or were being pursued by an eviler race and were forced here. Yet, through our ridiculous notions that different appearances, languages, or mannerisms immediately deem one wicked or unwanted, we instinctively turn to violence. The race of Men can be quite ignorant. As it is, we are in the middle of it now."

Rupert looked sickly while the Duke simply nodded silent agreement.

"Constable, tell the people to arm themselves but to remain indoors. Have them barricade stoutly as best they can. I wish to avoid further bloodshed, if possible. Do not tell them what we have found or speak of danger. Tell them the actions are merely precautionary," instructed the Duke.

Rupert nodded, but my eyes turned toward the darkened forest. "They will discover the truth sooner than not," I warned. "Things of this nature do not stay secret for long."

———————

Little convincing was needed for Byron to post watches facing the four cardinal directions. One lookout would be high atop the meeting house, another, the magistrate's office, yet another, the roof of the inn, and finally, within the boughs of the ancient elm tree on the western edge of town. We persuaded many of the elderly to abandon their homes and flee to the neighboring village with our aid. However, if we failed this night, it would be of little consequence in saving their lives as all may fall sooner than later.

For the most part, Balnorvia comprises peasants, farmers, shopkeepers, librarians, craftsmen, and the like. Residents are both young and old, emphasizing that their beloved home stands primarily defenseless. The former robust supply of more youthful and middle-aged men had been greatly diminished due to the last brutal war five years ago.

In this instance, the villagers would, due to lack of training and stark fear, eventually arm themselves with rolling pins, pitchforks, club-like pieces of wood, or rusty old swords that had not seen a whetstone in some years. The richest, who display wealth like spoiled children, bore a musket or shotgun. But to stand against such numbers as I imagined would come against them was akin to having a single match to set alight a room of candles. After all, what could these folks do against such vileness? They would likely huddle tightly under a kitchen table, in a dank cellar, or in a bedroom closet, unable to stop their terrified wails and moans from giving away their hiding spots.

Time passed, with the hours of dusk being the most frightening. With regret, I considered the villagers. Though still a mystery, what was to come would likely not end well. Seeing firsthand what these creatures could do made my blood curdle like soured milk.

Admittedly, I feared for my safety, wondering if wits alone could prove sufficient ammunition to remain alive until the end, whenever that came.

I waited for brooding night to hide the day as nagging, breathless tension grew in my chest. I had hoped to thoroughly examine the alien corpse but knew preparing the townsfolk was paramount, and the autopsy would need to wait.

Once the sun descended, the village turned from its usual pleasant appearance to a grossly disturbing atmosphere. It was most disconcerting. Families still ran wildly about to shelter together with friends or relatives. Many paused to gawk toward the gloomy, fog-entrenched mountains. Listening to the murmured gossip, I learned this was not normal, especially considering how the murky cloud swirled and moved.

There was a lot of muttering and more than a few skeptical looks cast my way, all of which I ignored. The evidence was clear and supported my few conclusions to this point. Not to mention, there was no denying the alien body, even though it had not been revealed as of yet. The villagers were told marauding invaders were closing in. We did not disclose the fact they were from another world.

The townsfolk grew to openly criticize my motives as I stood nearby, peering into the surrounding hills. Their behavior was childish but ordinary. After all, sheer terror takes hold of folks in different ways. Some soil themselves, while others flee or become frozen in dread. But a particular lot always finds a ridiculous need to voice their opinion, no matter how idiotic it may be—like Rupert and his wild boar theory.

Finally, after much pointless yammering, some men refused to be shut inside. They moved off in all directions to do what they could. Fouling things up even further was a distinct possibility, I thought. I had intended to tell those who stayed behind what would be coming for them, but they quickly dispersed beforehand.

A glance at my pocket watch showed it near the eight o'clock hour. The invaders would come soon. I sensed it. Looking to the windows, I saw many wide eyes peeking back, likely in place to watch the terrible events unfold. This is a characteristic trait in which humans find perverse pleasure, or fright, by watching twisted events unfold. There is an abhorrent sickness to it all.

I looked again in the direction the bickering fools had gone. They would be useless, the first to die once the creatures arrived, leaving only a slim few men to turn the tide. If that was even possible.

High above, evening clouds sundered to reveal a brilliant gibbous moon. Twinkling stars showed themselves as if coming to our aid, though I doubted they would ensure our survival.

Before finishing my thought, it began. The world seemed to burst apart as screams and clashing of weapons erupted from the westerly part of town. I bolted towards the sound with Byron by my side. Surprisingly, Rupert kept pace, as well. Fear proves to be the greatest motivator, I have said often. Hence, the emotion gave tireless, mighty legs to the petrified constable.

Less than two minutes passed before we arrived at the scene. Three men lay about in varying stages of agony. All were missing one limb or another, cut neatly away by sharp blades. Or perhaps removed by some weapon of unknown design or origin. Either way, the wounds were made with impressive precision. Around them, in the former remnants of a battle circle, lay five more brave enough to stand against the enemy tide or foolish enough not to heed my advice. I could not decide which. Regardless, they had already met their fate.

Adding to my foreboding was the sight of the poor young lad standing watch from above, who now lay amongst the dead. Slashed and torn, his body was scattered throughout the tree boughs like the previous corpses. His head was missing. My guess was it had been taken. Whether it is a trophy, a souvenir, or some otherworldly science experiment, I dare not say.

These creatures must have the agility of chimpanzees, I thought. To scale a tree and attack the young man in such a brief time was astounding and utterly frightening.

As other men arrived, running about shouting and hurrying past in various panicked states, I realized the horrible danger we had led ourselves into. I yelled for them to disperse to retake their posts, but again, they did not listen. Grief and terror had removed their sense.

Meanwhile, in an admirable strategy, the creatures slunk steadily from the thickest woods to form a loose circle about us. For a brief moment, a spark of hope ignited in my heart for a peaceful resolution. Unfortunately, I deemed it likely the dead villagers had done as previously thought. They had attacked the creatures once they crashed nearby. Now, revenge seemed to be on the alien's minds as their circle tightened quickly with determination.

I stood confounded. Neither my scientific background nor affinity for logic could help me. Never had I envisioned my end coming within the borders of Balnorvia.

"Run!" I shouted. "Form a wedge and follow me. Now, you damned fools!"

Pulling my pistol, I charged forward with Rupert and Byron. The men, seeing a bit of hope, followed. They raised a loud ruckus as they brandished their crude weapons. Some wiser ones grabbed up dead men's swords or pikes to charge by our side, and suddenly, the seemingly insurmountable odds fell away.

Hope sprang in my bosom as I fired a single shot. One hideous eye was extinguished. As the creature collapsed, the others froze for an instant. To all appearances, they were surprised by the sound of gunfire. Again, I squeezed the trigger. Another invader fell with a brief shriek of death. The awful noise it made prickled my skin.

The aliens' hesitation was all we needed as our small force clashed against their sizeable lines with vigor. Weapons met, shouts rose, screams filled the air, and death found us again. Less fortunate men fell away at my sides. I fired until my pistol was empty, then seized an alien sword and fought on.

The creatures were closing, yet we held our own. I hacked another monster to my left, then rounded at the sound of a hideous shriek in time to see Rupert lunge before me as a steel blade passed through his shoulder. The foolish halfwit saved my life.

In response, I beheaded the creature, then stooped to seize the constable's collar to drag him to safety. To my relief, two older men appeared. We grabbed the heavy man and hauled him forward. Finally, we broke through the creatures' defenses, though I do not know how.

Still outnumbered, I shouted over my shoulder at the remaining men. "Retreat! Retreat!"

To my shock, Rupert steadied himself, still bleeding in a flowing stream, and ran alongside me. Perhaps there was more in him than I had previously admitted.

The thinning line of survivors surged forward, again grabbing superior weapons when able. The creatures' abysmal screams and chattering language filled the air as they gave chase. Onward, we ran, finding refuge in a sturdy barn. One man bolted the lock as I turned to inspect our surroundings. I thanked the gods for bestowing these folks with such notable building skills.

As luck would have it, a surviving member was the local doctor. He tended to the wounded as best he could, but so numerous were they that it became evident most would not survive the night. I whispered in his ear to tend to Rupert quickly, for I was concerned about his health. Meaning the man did save me from certain death.

Outside, the intruders hacked and hewed the boards to little avail. Some, seen through the narrow slats, skittered on the sides and roof like giant blue spiders. Their claws gripped and held while their light bodies clambered all around us.

Amidst the grave panic and confusion, not to mention the sickly smell of blood and flesh, a hand gripped my shoulder with sudden force. My heart nearly stopped from dread. Thankfully, Henry, the delivery lad from the castle, had seemingly appeared from thin air.

I smiled as best I could. "Where did you come from, my boy? How is it you are here?" I pointed to the ground. "Hurry now, for there is not much time. I need a quick answer."

"Sir, it's a tunnel. There." He indicated a large trap door betwixt two stout pillars. It stood wide open. "It's an ol' escape tunnel used during the wars. To evade the enemy, my lord. We all helped dig it from end to end."

Delight lit my heart, tempered by anxiety. "Where does it lead?"

"Outta town, coming up near the large rock outcropping in the forest to the east," he said, pushing his chin in the direction.

I took his shoulders with both hands and dropped to my knees. "Henry, my boy, if we survive this, there are five silver pieces for you. In fact, these people should build a statue of your likeness in the square. May the gods bless you for being so brave." Rising, I spun and waved an arm. "This way, lads! Save yourselves. I will not leave Rupert here to fend for himself. I shall stay behind. Quietly, now. Off you go."

The pounding, shrieking, and scurrying continued around us as I realized the doctor had stayed behind. I clamped a hand on his arm and nodded my appreciation.

As the weary men lowered themselves by use of ladder, I tasked the young man with one more valiant deed. He was to procure medical supplies from the doctor's office by any means necessary and return stealthily, as quick as able. He agreed and set off, returning some long minutes later.

Leaving behind the constable, who had lapsed into unconsciousness due to blood loss, I took to the tunnels with Henry. The brave, competent doctor stayed behind to tend to Rupert and the other wounded.

The frightened, fatigued men were waiting when we emerged from the distant woods. There, as the saying goes, we rallied in hopes of turning the tables. Though weary from battle, we slunk into town to lay our trap, encircling the creatures still attacking the barn. They slashed, hacked, and pulled at the thick planks, but anger and blood lust would not prevail against such a fortress-like structure. Yet, they had nearly broken through in spots. Time was clearly of the essence if we wished to save the trapped men.

A few hand commands passed down the line was all it took, and our final charge—the bloodiest, most costly, yet most successful—took the aliens totally unawares. Screaming and shrieking, they disappeared into the forest as dawn greyed the sky. But the price was staggering.

Nearly half the remaining men had fallen during the last melee. And the town's survival did not come without all the horror, blood, and fear close-quarter combat brings.

Since I have long since pondered the exact reason for the aliens' abrupt scattering and entertained several such ideas. All or none may have played a role in our victory. We will never know if they hid from the light, possibly overly sensitive due to their singular eye, or if our perseverance and trickery in battle stymied them. It would not be the first time ingenuity prevailed against superior forces.

As the sun climbed higher, women and children poured from the buildings. There were gasps and twisted expressions. I did not blame them but wished they had not witnessed the abhorrent state of things. It is certainly no place for children. To their credit, many quickly directed their little ones inside as others wept and moaned over hewed and bloodied loved ones.

Stretcher-bearers bore Rupert from the barn, stopping near the commotion. Despite being white from blood loss, he looked no worse for the wear. I took his hand and smiled at him.

"I am sorry," I said as his sausage-like fingers closed round my hand. "I misjudged you. You saved my life—a debt I cannot repay. Perhaps, when this is over, you could return to the city with me. I require an assistant. Further"—I looked down at the young boy standing at my shoulder—"I deem Henry stout of heart, too. He may accompany us, should he wish."

For a fearful moment, I wondered if the man would burst from joy. He nearly leaped from his stretcher, causing a great deal of mumbling and complaining from his handlers. I steadied him.

"Now, now. At this rate, you will kill yourself simply by standing. I shall see you again before too long. Rest well, Rupert." I turned to the boy. "Come along, Henry, there is more to do. We are needed."

The lad followed, a wide grin forming on his lips as we strode off.

Then, a horribly frightening moment came to pass. The ground shook, and thunderous rumbling noises filled our ears. Many fell to their knees to cower. I saw abnormal movement from the corner of my eye and rounded to face it.

Though the world was frantic around me, silence prevailed as several black orbs drifted overhead. The feeling was one akin to having your ears plugged with water. Normal sounds dissipated, twisting into ugly scores of sounds that scattered my senses. I drew back as the spheres hovered low—directly overhead. Would these beings unleash a weapon yet unseen? Undoubtedly, if they could manage space travel, it would not be outside the realm of likelihood. Were these my final moments? Had we escaped a deadly attack only to die gawking in the very end?

The ships began to shimmer as if wrapped in rising heat. There, they hovered for several moments as the town watched with bated breath. Then, as rapidly as they appeared, they vanished in streaks of blazing blue light with a swishing sound.

"My lord, do you think the ships will return?" asked Henry softly.

I raised an eyebrow. "I certainly hope not. If they do, I believe there will be many more of them, and they learned from this experience." My gaze raked over the desolate, blood-stained village where humanity had only just prevailed. "Their next visit could be far different. And the outcome may not be a favorable one."

———

Later that morning, as the cleanup process was ongoing, I learned, much to my heartfelt dismay, that the Duke had fallen in combat during the western attack. For a man I barely knew, sadness returned to my heart. He was a fine fellow and a bright intelligence this world desperately needed.

During the laborious work, Wilford the butler found me to hand over an official letter embossed with Byron's official wax seal. Opening it, I found yet another surprise since entering this strange little village.

The Duke, valuing my reputation and knowledge, deemed me his heir, gifting me his castle and position. His twin sons had been killed during the war, and he had no other to claim his chair. His wife passed years ago from typhus, and the pair had no other inheritors born to them. As noted upon my arrival, the man must have had an unspoken premonition of his premature death and prepared for it in a way he deemed most fitting.

So it was, within my newly appointed title, I vowed to travel the region in pursuit of unnatural, terrifying phenomena, wherever they may lead us. I say 'us' since Rupert and Henry, as promised, would become my assistants. After all, they proved their worth, and I was in their debt.

I transcribe this tale now to warn people against strange events. Not all things seen are figments of your imagination. Some hold unspeakable evil. Soon, these creatures may return to sweep us away like we clear dust from our floors. I pray to the gods I do not see those days, but if you should encounter such danger, send a message to the Duke of Balnorvia, and I shall answer, if able.

Best of luck. Question everything.

Signed: Gerrit van Egmond, Duke of Balnorvia

THE PERFECT PLAN

A s daylight faded, yielding to broadening darkness, the clouds opened briefly. The storm had rolled past. Overhead, the star-filled night embraced Destiny like a lover.

She wore her usual gothic style: lace arm sleeves, fishnet stockings, studded choker, and knee-high boots. Naturally, like her lengthy hair, all were black, save for the purple velvet skirt that ended just above her knees. Her full lips were covered in darkly shaded lipstick. Black circles and heavy eyeliner adorned her eyes. Her nails were raven-colored.

Anticipation soared. Knowing this night had finally arrived felt like a drug coursing through her veins. Her plan seemed flawless, but only time would tell. In truth, she had only sent four invitations, each with specific instructions to keep the party and its location secret, saying it was meant to be a surprise of sorts. The recipients had no idea how many students would be present.

Undoubtedly, her guests would be on time. Whenever sex, alcohol, and drugs were promised—as they were in this case—people seemed to magically appear. Tonight would be no different. She counted on it.

The house looked perfect. It was more of a castle than not. The enormous vertical structure had been erected during the fifteenth century, with rose windows, towering buttresses, and pointed arches. Each sizeable stained-glass window was flawless, no doubt painstakingly painted by hand to reveal their multicolored glory. Not one pane was broken even after all these years.

Great gargoyles, mute in their unending observations, perched along the towering outer edges. The stony figures peered on with rigid faces. Rainwater still dripped from their open mouths.

Next were the grotesques who mocked humanity with their twisted facades. The hideously ugly, even disgusting, distorted forms were a mystery in origin. Some bore human faces, others were plainly animals, and yet more, a combination of the two. Their figures were strategically placed in stone corbels, keystones, and friezes. Unlike gargoyles, they were fashioned to scare and protect, at least if the legends were true.

Destiny wished to see them more clearly. The clouds, which had begun to thicken, suddenly parted as if in response from the higher powers. Pale moonlight trickled through the cloudy veil, touching upon the granite faces.

She loved them all. They were her favorite part of the old castle. What would they say if they could retell tales from the previous five hundred years? What sort of things had they seen over the centuries, she wondered. Wars? Death? Happiness? There was no way to know.

Cloud cover reconverged to conceal the bright, first-quarter moon. Destiny moved down the graveled lane, ensuring the 'Party Inside' signs were still well-placed. From a distance, she studied the castle. It was sheer loveliness. No matter how often she came here, it looked as wonderous as the first time she saw it.

The castle was styled after Transitoria, Nero's ancient home, aptly named the House of Passages. Destiny wished she could live within its walls. Though exploring the corridors for many months, she had yet to reach each room, walk the endless halls, or discover any ancient, hidden secrets that she was convinced lay within.

"You are a masterpiece," she said softly. "Workmanship like yours has long since been forgotten."

It saddened her the old ways were dying with each passing day, replaced by people living in agitated, frenzied states, complete with modern phobias and laundry lists of mental issues. Even with her belief in the ancient gods and their evil counterparts, this world was pushing humanity to negative consequences. Just last month, her father paid for her to see a psychiatrist for having conversations with inanimate objects. Though she hated the idea of speaking to a shrink, she gave in to keep the family peace.

Dr. Treadmill, as Destiny named her due to her constant repetition of things the girl cared little for, said the condition was named *personification.* The affliction led to pretending inanimate objects were living things or people. In the doctor's words, once a patient—Destiny hated being called that—applied human attributes to inanimate objects, nature, animals, or abstract concepts, they were clinically insane or suffering from personification. In some of the worst instances, the afflicted created dramatic stories about their invented friends' social roles, emotions, and intentions.

Destiny did no such thing. She spoke to her friends, and they answered. Even from an early age, she knew to keep her secret just that—secret. Otherwise, she would wear a stiff canvas jacket, be pumped full of medication, or live in a padded room. Perhaps all three. During her sessions, she had taken great care to appear anxious yet demure, shyly seeking the help her parents longed for her to have. Yet in private, she spoke long into the night to her many acquaintances, to the voices others insisted only existed in her mind. Pure and utter gibberish, she thought. She had no intention of stopping because a doctor believed the entire scenario was a whim of fancy.

She grasped the door handle, pausing to take a long breath, then slowly let it out. The heavy wooden door opened noiselessly before she crossed the threshold and closed herself inside. She looked about. Truly magnificent, she thought again. She ran her fingers lovingly over the walls and railings and went to the second floor to wait.

Some twenty minutes passed before two cars rumbled down the long driveway to park in the uppermost portion of the graveled cul-de-sac. Destiny's back straightened as she looked on from high above while the participants eased from their cars in fine fashion to amble toward the door.

"Looks like we're the first ones here," said Tim, the average-looking, stocky football player. He brushed the hair from his eyes with an imperial sweep of his hand as if preparing to pose for a magazine cover. But the trait he was most known for was being a cruel bully. Thanks to a combination of status and size, no one stood up to him. His twisted, sociopathic behavior had gone unchecked for years.

Conversely, Chad liked finer things, and they were easy to obtain with absurdly wealthy parents. He drove expensive cars, wore fine clothes, and spent money at every opportunity. Though he treated women like matches—using them once before discarding them forever—he was a smooth talker and could connive his way into a girl's pants with little effort, especially if they knew he was rich, which covered nearly every female in town.

Bedding women was a game to him. And if that game went awry, as it sometimes did, his parents would ensure any pending trouble vanished, usually by placing wads of cash into the right hands and making the issue vanish like a puff of smoke.

"Why are we standing around? I'm freezing," complained Hailey. She perfectly matched Chad's affluent personality—an offensive snob who envisioned herself far above others. In reality, she was a classless gold digger who would sleep with anyone who could support her fake, decadent lifestyle. It was apparent why she paired herself with Chad. And everyone knew it.

Jessica, though she preferred Jess, was a small, redheaded thief and another user of men when it suited her needs, which was daily. Her methods differed little from Hailey's, except that she rarely slept with her targeted victims. She merely created close relationships by quickly confessing her feelings of love, then after a short time, would purloin anything of value before disappearing from her victim's lives entirely. To date, she has never worked a day in her life. Her belongings were either gifted or came from ill-begotten gains.

Destiny sucked in a breath as Samantha—Sammy to her friends—exited Chad's car. Dressed casually in her favorite boots, blue blouse, and slim-fit jeans, the girl was attractive and sweet. She was not supposed to be here. Undoubtedly, the others were not her kind. The only reason Sammy would be invited along was because they owed her. She actively helped them pass classes, doing work for five students counting herself.

Without her, the imbeciles would be heading home to their parents as disgraced failures. They needed her. But she seemed invisible this night, like any other when she was near. When she closed the car door, the others were already strolling to the house.

Groaning at the unexpected dilemma while hoping her guests had not disclosed the party to others, Destiny wavered momentarily. Then she rose from her seat on the stairs. She could still go on with her plan. Sammy's presence was of little consequence. She would simply be dealt with when the time was right.

Destiny moved to the thick wooden railing overlooking the first floor. When observed from above, the beautiful archaic tiles caught her breath. The pattern, undetectable while standing upon its surface, was far more intricate and lovely from a raised vantage point. Then, the floor became not just one of colored wonder but formed the face of a large raven surrounded by strange writings and unknown symbols. Appreciation for the ancient craftsmanship made her shiver with happiness, as did the knowledge of what would soon occur.

The five students entered, crossing the threshold of a world they had never imagined. They closed the door and gawked at the sight.

Chad whistled a shrill sound. "Dig this old place! I would live here. It suits my style. Why haven't I seen this before?"

"Because you're always too busy shopping or screwing to do anything else," snipped Jess.

Chad scowled at her. "At least I can afford to buy my stuff and don't need to steal it."

Jess flushed red and displayed her middle finger. "Asshole."

"Knock it off," said Tim, guiding Jess away. "You sound like a couple of five-year-old children."

"Time has come," whispered Destiny, still unnoticed as she caressed the railing with her fingertips.

At that moment, sounds akin to grating stone or heavy objects moving over granite with great effort echoed within the hall.

"What's that noise?" grumbled Tim, puffing his chest out as if preparing for an attack.

"It's just this old house," said Chad. "Relax, dude. Do you need someone to hold your hand?" He reached out only to have his mocking effort slapped away.

"Don't be rude to my man," snapped Hailey to the football star. "He'll kick your ass if you disrespect him again." She took Chad's arm and snuggled against it. "Won't you, baby?"

Chad blushed and swallowed hard. "No need for any of that garbage. We're here to have fun and get stoned. Let's find this party."

Tim snorted, then chuckled at the pair. "See, you can have common sense when you need it. Good choice."

The noises, forgotten in a moment of happy thought, returned, permeating the walls like a disease testing entrance to a new host. Scraping and clawing sounds rebounded within the chambered room from all directions, even above. The companions' eyes went toward the ceiling only to land on Destiny standing patiently at the top of the stairs.

"What is *she* doing here," said Jess, pointing as she met her antagonist's dark eyes.

Destiny curtsied, then nodded slowly. "At your service. Unfortunately for you, I am tonight's party host."

"What's your game, freak. You shouldn't be here. This party is for normal people," said Tim, wagging a stiff finger in her direction before checking over his shoulder, ensuring the others laughed. He enjoyed being the center of attention. "I'm going to teach you a lesson and . . ."

Pounding on the large front doors halted his words.

Jess sprang to Tim's side. Her eyes shot wide with fear. "What is that? Make it stop. It's freaking me out." Her gaze went to Destiny, and again, she pointed an accusing finger. "This is your doing, bitch."

Destiny laughed. "For once in your miserable existence, you've stated the truth. Oh, another surprise is that you are absolutely right." She descended a few steps, focusing on Jess. "Do you remember stealing my new laptop from my workstation? Or have you forgotten how you swiped the money from my gym locker while I showered? My friend saw you."

Jess scoffed. "Liar! No one saw me take . . ." Her words faltered, and she blushed, knowing she had been caught. She hung her head, remaining behind Tim as if he were a shield protecting her from her deceits.

"Shut up, you moron. You're making things worse," said Hailey to the redhead.

Jess's face flushed. She stepped forward with a hand raised, only to flinch away as the pounding, much louder now, returned with force. Chad stepped between the girls and Tim, closing out their huddled circle. Sammy stood alone and forgotten, cowering in the shadows behind a large pillar.

"I'm leaving. This is complete bullshit," declared Chad in a shaken voice. He faced Destiny. "You're no one special and can't keep us here. Screw you." He balled up his fist and thrust it upward.

"I wouldn't open that door if you plan to live more than a few seconds, rapist," she replied. Her last word hung in the air with a viscous feeling.

A soft gasp escaped from Sammy as she slipped farther into the darkened corner.

The room fell into eerie silence.

Hailey backed away from the group, arms wrapped around herself. A look of confusion and disbelief registered on her face. "What is she talking about?"

Chad's expression morphed into one of forced innocence. His voice raised an octave. "I . . . I . . . don't know. She's crazy. Everyone knows it." He pushed his chin in her direction. "Look at her! She's a nut job. Not to mention a certified devil lover."

"Surely you remember the night you caught me coming home late from the library," Destiny said, descending a bit farther. Her tone was soft and even. "That poor little thing between your legs must have been lonely. Maybe it got tired of seeing your hand so often. Your mistake was being stupid enough to wear that expensive necklace your folks gave you. You know, the one I tore from your neck as you raped me. I still have it." She patted her pocket. "By the way, I hope the wounds I gave you never heal." Her fingers curled into a claw-shape as they gently raked across her throat.

Hailey's terrified eyes darted toward Chad's neck. The scars were plain to see. "You told me you did that wrestling with Tim. You said it was an accident."

Tim scoffed and held up both hands in a gesture of innocence. "Leave me out of it."

"Shut up, both of you," snapped Chad.

"What do you want?" Jess shouted toward the staircase.

More pounding and scratching battered the air. A howl escaped. The friends exchanged nervous stares.

Destiny resumed her slow descent. "And you, sweet little Hailey, thank you so much for posting those naked, photoshopped pics of me. They really got everyone talking." The goth girl frowned for the first time. "Too bad you're too stupid to know about I.P. addresses and how to track them. Did you think I couldn't find out who did put that fake garbage online?"

Hailey's face drained of color. "It . . . it was a joke." She laughed lightly, sounding wholly unsure of herself. "I didn't mean . . ."

"And muscle man, Tim," Destiny interrupted while halting on a particularly creaky step. "You laid hands on my best friend. You must've felt pretty tough slapping a girl around until she needed a hospital. Very bad form, dipshit." Her eyes narrowed. "I will be sure you die most horribly."

"Wha . . . wha . . . what is she talking about?" stammered Jess. She gritted her teeth and spun. "I've had enough!" she hollered, meeting Destiny's cold stare. "Let us go, or else."

"Or else what?" asked Destiny with her usual steady calm. "It is time to introduce you to my friends and lay down the rules. They are simple, really—even for all of you. If you survive their wrath until dawn, you can go about your miserable lives with my blessings."

"What friends? Your stupid Goth friends? I'll kick *all* their asses," proclaimed Tim, pounding a fist into his other palm. "What are they going to do, slap me to death." He laughed again. The others did not.

Destiny ignored him.

"And if we're caught? Then what?" asked Hailey, her eyes darting over the room with a frightened stare. "What will happen?"

"Let's just say all your past transgressions will be absolved." Destiny smiled again. "By the way, if any of my words are too large, I can give you a minute to look them up on your phones." She chuckled. "Oh, wait, there's no cell service here. Never mind, then."

In unison, as if the concept was foreign or totally forgotten, all four freed their phones to stare at the screens. Hailey raised hers high, then moved around the room to no avail. Chad's composure slipped with every second no bars appeared. Anger mixed with desperation edged onto their faces.

"That's it! I'm going to break your neck, you filthy . . ." Tim charged the steps.

Destiny clapped her hands to gain his attention as he rocketed closer. "I want you to meet one of my imaginary friends. At least, that's what my family calls them—imaginary." Another wicked grin graced her face. "Oh, Vuzarin, could you please lend a hand," she asked sweetly.

The large stone gargoyle stepped into the light to spread his great wings for an instant. Shrieks of fear rose from below. Again, the others trembled. Tim, looking far less brave, quickly retreated to rejoin them.

"What the hell is that!" cried Chad. He recoiled, drawing both hands tightly to his chest in dread.

"It's a guy in a suit. Nothing like that exists. So fake!" said Hailey, waving a dismissive hand as she rolled her eyes.

"I . . . I . . . I'm not so sure," stuttered Jess.

"It seems the proverbial cat is out of the bag." Destiny turned to Sammy. "You have no part in this. I suggest you run to find cover, then stay there."

As quickly as her legs would carry her, Sammy scurried into deep shadows down a long hall. The girl needed no prompting to save herself. Destiny watched her flee toward the east wing, marking it in her mind.

Hailey and Chad attempted to follow, but a low growl from Vuzarin froze them. Clawed feet advanced before Destiny lay a hand on the gargoyle's massive shoulder.

"This wonderful being and some of *his* friends will hunt you until dawn. You will be free to go once the sun rises above the horizon. Providing you survive, of course." Another malicious smile. "May your deaths be as excruciatingly painful as what you have put me through this year." She swept a hand before her. "I suggest running instead of wasting time with your pointless words or thoughts of screaming."

The quaking human prey, hurriedly understanding their dilemma, fled from sight, scattering into dimly lit hallways.

Taking Vuzarin's grey face in her hands, Destiny lowered her voice. "Tell the others the girl in the blue blouse must remain unharmed. I will hunt her myself."

With a graveled voice, Vuzarin spoke. "As you wish, Mistress. The sentence of death has been uttered, and so shall it be bestowed upon those who have done you harm." With a quick movement, the gargoyle bound over the railing, spread his wings again, then glided to the main floor to land with another shaking thud. Throwing his horned head back, Vuzarin let loose a call that resounded through the castle's innards.

Doors and windows flung wide as both gargoyle and grotesque alike arrived in answer. Vuzarin issued orders in a tongue even Destiny did not comprehend, though she recognized the meaning clearly enough. The die had been cast in favor of death and destruction.

Chad ran as panic narrowed his vision. Hailey kept pace beside him. Doors and hallways flew past as they sprinted the passageway. He glanced over his shoulder only to see Vuzarin bearing down on them. To his horror, an unfamiliar sensation gripped his soul—terror unlike any he dreamed possible. It was not the edge-of-your-seat intrigue one gets from a book or movie. Rather, one that scrambled his thoughts, sped his heart to the point of bursting, and in its full appreciation of his predicament, made him lightheaded, nearing the point of fainting. Yet, he ran on while gripping Hailey's hand.

"These things are toying with us," he said, huffing along in a sprint. His inclination was perfectly correct. It was a cat-and-mouse game with no apparent means of escape. Only barred windows and locked doors greeted them.

With every new glimpse of their hunter, who steadily drew closer, Hailey urged them into dimly shaded corners to hide behind flowing drapes or bulky furniture. Skidding around a corner to temporarily lose sight of their pursuer, the duo ducked behind a long, high-backed sofa to wait. But Chad could not remain still for long.

Though Vuzarin slowed, another pursuer—a grotesque with a large club in his sizeable, gnarled hand—lumbered into view to join the chase. The human pair, entirely unnerved by the commotion, bolted again.

Chad ignored Hailey's frantic protests as he hurtled forward without logic or a solid plan. His hand shook loose, and Hailey fell behind. He slid to a stop, this time behind a massive pillar. His breath was ragged. Hailey arrived seconds later, clutching her side.

Odd sounds drew their attention upward to where several grotesques clung to the large wooden ceiling beams. They shadowed the fleeing humans from above. Gargoyles waited patiently, mockingly, at each end of the hall. Vuzarin approached. This pursuit had reached a pinnacle.

"I have a plan," Chad announced with confidence. He took her sweaty palm in his. "Do you trust me?"

Hailey contemplated his question for a moment. "Y . . . y . . . yes," she stammered unconvincingly. "I trust you."

"Then come on," he answered, tugging her hand as he dashed from cover again.

Hailey resisted, trying to break his grip, but it was too tight. "You're running toward them, you idiot," she cried.

Chad's heartbeat rang in his ears, drowning out Hailey's screams and objections as he pulled her along. At the end of the hall stood Vuzarin, eyes gleaming.

Forty feet separated prey and predator. Thirty. Twenty. Ten. At last, Chad stopped, jerking Hailey to a halt. Before she could speak, he took her face in his hands and kissed her warmly.

"I'm sorry. But I'm way more important than you are," Chad said, shoving her into the gargoyle's waiting arms.

Hailey's scream never came, nor did Chad witness the unseemly sight. At that moment, as she was torn to pieces, he sprinted past. Blood splattered the walls, floor, and portions of the ceiling. Some landed on his clothing, though he took no notice.

Chad's feet slapped the stone floor as he raced to the front doors to grasp the large iron handles and pull for all his worth. They moved nary an inch. Again and again, he tried, but to no avail. The heavy entries were solid and impenetrable. Hope drained away as the scraping sound of stone reached his ears. Vuzarin had returned.

Chad fought back tears of helplessness. He would be a victim, like an animal caught in a python's coils—holding, tightening, squeezing until all signs of his life were extinguished. The floor vibrated as he turned, backing into a marbled corner as the gargoyle slowly advanced. Too petrified to make a sound, his eyes widened as the living stone creature swiped a long, clawed limb outward. Chad's partially crushed head rolled across the floor with a revolting slapping sound, coming to rest in a corner.

———

Jess discovered a seldom-used hallway. She crept its length as silently as her stylish boots would allow. Cringing after each footfall, she slunk forward. She tested every door, but each one rejected her, forcing her deeper into despair as choices slimmed. Helplessness welled in her, knowing none would come even if she cried for help.

Soon, to her surprise, with a twist of a large brass doorknob, the last door opened to the outside world. The scent of fresh rain filled her nostrils as she rushed to the cars, ecstatic. No one would hear her footfalls now. She felt safe.

With one hand on the car door, she rounded to flip a middle finger toward the castle. "Take that, you stupid bitch! Who's trapped now!"

Another obscene gesture. "I'm telling everyone what you've done. You'll be in prison forever, you psycho!"

Jess flung open the door and slid into the seat to search for the keys, only to be disappointed. They were gone. She tried the other car, as well, but met the same results. She cursed. With a quick hop, she was on her feet, running toward the road. Within fifty yards, a slow dawning came to her frantic mind. Something was following. Should I look back, she wondered.

Using all her willpower, she pressed forward, her thick legs striding with speed one would not expect from an unathletic person. But monstrous fear can become a tremendous motivator.

Just then, a grotesque bolted from the woods to tangle in the girl's legs, biting and clawing at her ankles. Jess screamed and tripped, her face crushing hard against the graveled driveway. Her broken nose erupted with crimson spray. Small rocks cut and tore her flesh. With a grunt, as tears blurred her vision, she spewed blood from her mouth. Two teeth followed as she spat again.

Her hands clawed the gravel as she struggled to a half-seated position. She looked up.

A shriek tore from her throat as the man-troll, Cractow, closed down on her. More followed. Her pleas and screams were cut short as the creatures swarmed, their hard, stony fists falling in a repeated frenzy, reducing her body to a pile of bloody clothing and a crimson stain on the graveled drive. Even her bones were flattened to tiny fragments after the thrashing.

Cractow snatched up the stained clothing and lumbered toward the castle.

———————

Destiny bound down the stairs and moved toward the great wooden doors of the east wing. Horrific shouts and shrieks filled the hall with a pleasing sound—revenge. Her plan was working perfectly.

Wild, frantic yelps drew nearer as the sound of running met her ears. Destiny whirled to see Tim following in a rattled state. He was disheveled, sweaty, and looked mentally unbalanced.

Another gargoyle, Vabex, was close behind. Destiny swore she could see a smile on the stone face—the creature was enjoying her game. Clearly, she could have easily finished the pursuit. A quick flap of her wings would have brought her within reach of Tim—yet she chased him farther on.

Tim dashed in Destiny's direction. Ten feet away, he dropped to his knees.

"Please," he begged, his hands clasped in the Christian prayer position, "I'll do anything you say. Just don't let that thing kill me." He glanced over his shoulder as Vabex suddenly towered over him. Bending forward, the creature's face came within inches of his head. Her breath stirred his mused hair. Tim soiled himself as tears rolled down his cheeks.

Destiny raised a hand. Vabex straightened and paused, stone eyes fixed on her victim as the girl considered his fate. There was no question he should die, but how?

Extending her hands wide, the goth girl brought them together quickly to clap once. Thinking he had been granted reprieve, Tim sprang to his feet in joy, unaware the gargoyle parroted the girl's actions, spreading her clawed limbs before slapping them shut.

The young man's head exploded like a balloon pierced by a sharp needle. His headless body fell with a thud as blood spilled from his corpse.

Vabex displayed a thin smile. "He was the last. It is done."

Destiny stepped forward to hug her friend. "Thank you," she whispered. "I must find Sammy now." Rounding back toward the wing, the girl ran on, calling her friend's name. "Sammy, you are safe. You have my word. Come out. It's over."

Terrible disappointment welled in her stomach, thinking Sammy had escaped somehow. What would this mean for her? They had been friends for a long time, but Destiny could not ignore the burning issue. Things could turn out poorly if the girl told of this evening's events.

Ready to concede defeat and return to the main hall, Destiny halted when a voice came from a shadowed corner to her left.

"I . . . I . . . I don't want to die," stammered Sammy.

Destiny ran to her. "Why are you here? You do not belong with these fools."

She opened both arms to embrace her. Sammy flinched, then slowly stepped forward to bury her face in Destiny's shoulder, arms wrapping around her waist. Her eyes went to the headless body. She shuddered, then stepped back.

"I know," she replied. "I just wanted to fit in somewhere and thought maybe they would like me better if I hung out with them."

Destiny kissed her cheek tenderly. "You *do* belong somewhere." She pointed at the floor beside her. "Right here. I've waited for you to realize how much I want to be with you. I should have told you long ago. I'm sorry you had to find out this way."

Sammy kissed Destiny's lips. "It was my fault, too. I feel the same but didn't know how to tell you. I'm ready now." She squeezed Destiny's hand after another lingering look at the corpse. "I'm so glad he's gone." Her face soured. "I never knew he did that to you. I'm so sorry."

Destiny scowled. "He got what he deserved. No more forcing himself on women or grabbing them from the shadows." She jerked a thumb toward the headless body as they passed. "It all worked out in the end."

Moments passed before they entered the main hall. The creatures awaited their arrival.

Vuzarin tossed two objects onto the floor. They rolled like misshapen dice until they came to rest at the girls' feet. One was Hailey's head, her mouth still agape in an unfinished scream. Both eyes were wide open, staring upward. Tim's cranium lay next to it, tipped oddly since a good piece of the skull was absent. Nonetheless, there it was.

Cractow dropped the pile of blood-soaked clothing next to the heads. "This is the one who tried to escape. We caught her and pounded her like the flesh-thing she was."

"Your wishes have been fulfilled, Mistress," announced Traxium with a bow.

Destiny returned the gesture, then hugged each in turn, with Vuzarin last.

"Splendid work, my loyal, remarkable friends. I ask for no more than our continued alliance. You will remain in my life until I no longer draw breath." She glanced at a window. The sky was paling again. "Please return to your perches with my thanks. We shall be together soon, for I will not allow you to sit idly as time passes around you."

After bowing in unison, the creatures flung wide the doors to hurry away into the grey morning. The sound of grating stone returned as the beings settled onto their resting spots.

"The campus will be a much better place now," said Sammy as they descended the front steps and started down the drive. "And it sure takes a load off of my schedule."

Destiny laughed. "Perfect. Now, maybe you can spend more time with me."

Sammy leaned into her. "Great minds must think alike." She stopped in her tracks as if struck by a discovered error. "What about their cars?"

Destiny puffed air through her pursed lips. "It's the weekend. No one will even know they're missing until Monday at the earliest. We'll return tomorrow." She pointed to the statues. "Our friends can help us get rid of any evidence."

They kissed. Hand in hand, they walked away. Again, their eyes went to the gargoyles and grotesques. The girls smiled and waved, then headed for Destiny's car, hidden in the rear alcove. She parked there, knowing it would come in handy. It was all part of her plan. The perfect plan.

Made in the USA
Middletown, DE
05 November 2023

41884147R00106